TWO-MINUTE MYSTERIES COLLECTION

Two-Minute Mysteries
More Two-Minute Mysteries
Still More Two-Minute Mysteries

DONALD J. SOBOL

SCHOLASTIC INC.

New York Toronto London Auckland Sydney
Mexico City New Delhi Hong Kong Buenos Aires

ISBN 0-439-64383-X

Two-Minute Mysteries, ISBN 0-590-44787-4, Copyright © 1967 by Donald J. Sobol.; *More Two-Minute Mysteries*, ISBN 0-590-03454-5, Copyright © 1971 by Donald J. Sobol.; *Still More Two-Minute Mysteries*, ISBN 0-590-44786-6, Copyright © 1975 by Donald J. Sobol. All rights reserved. Published by Scholastic Inc. SCHOLASTIC and associated logos are trademarks and/or registered trademarks of Scholastic Inc.

12 11 10 9 8 7 6 5 4 3   4 5 6 7 8 9/0

Printed in the U.S.A.   40

First compilation printing, April 2004

CONTENTS

TWO-MINUTE MYSTERIES

For Gloria and Bill Keithan

The Case of the
Angry Chef

Hawkins, the marine, stared in amazement at Inspector Winters.

"I never heard of a restaurant called Pasquale's Pizzeria," he objected. "I wasn't ever in it, I didn't rob it, and I certainly didn't shoot anybody."

"A marine answering your description wounded the owner and cleaned out the cash register," said the inspector. "You didn't know?"

"Am I supposed to?" protested Hawkins. "There must be several thousand marines in this town."

"But only one was running along 42nd Street five minutes after the holdup," snapped the inspector.

"Sure I ran," retorted Hawkins. "Look, I was standing idly in a doorway wondering what to do when this fat guy wearing a white apron and chef's hat comes charging at me. He's waving a butcher knife and he's screaming, 'He shot the boss!' So I ran."

1

"You were innocent, but you ran?"

"He had that big knife."

"Then what did you do?"

"A cop saw us and grabbed me. It wasn't any use to argue. So I went back to the restaurant with the cop, and a couple of customers said I might be the marine who held up the place. They weren't sure."

That night Haledjian read the transcript of the questioning.

"Hawkins is your man," he said. "No mistake about it!"

How did Haledjian know?

Hawkins asserted he'd never heard of the restaurant or been in it. If true, he could not have gone "back" to it, as he said. A fatal slip of the tongue!

The Case of the
Attempted Murder

"Jack Alden's account of the attempted strangling of Mrs. McHenry is pretty farfetched," Inspector Winters told Dr. Haledjian. "Yet he passed a lie detector test.

"Alden drives a delivery truck for Best Cleaners," explained the inspector. "At five minutes before noon Tuesday he drove to the McHenry House and stopped the truck in the driveway.

"He spent about two minutes filling out his delivery reports for the morning. Then he got out with a dress and two suits.

"As he closed the cab door, he noticed his front wheels were parked on the garden hose which ran from an outlet by the garage around to the back of the house. Alden claims he got back into the truck and drove forward a few feet so that his engine was in the McHenry's empty garage.

"Here he noticed the door between the kitchen

3

and the garage was open. He saw Mrs. McHenry lying on the floor by the stove.

"He rushed to her, he says, and was trying to revive her when Mr. McHenry came through the open door of the garage.

"McHenry had taken the day off to water his backyard garden. He had been hosing down his flowerbeds and hedges for half an hour when he noticed the truck in his garage. He walked over to investigate.

"We can't get McHenry," concluded the inspector, "to state definitely whether he thinks Alden was trying to throttle his wife or revive her."

"No wonder the lie detector test didn't trap Alden!" said Haledjian.

Why not?

Because Alden told the truth.

Haledjian deduced that McHenry, while throttling his wife, had been surprised by the arrival of the deliveryman and had hurried to the backyard and his alibi of hosing his garden.

Had he been there all the time, he would have investigated why the water stopped flowing. The truck wheels were parked on the garden hose for "about two minutes," remember?

The Case of the
Attic Suicide

Motoring through Ashe City, Dr. Haledjian decided to drop in on his old friend, Carl Messner. At Messner's home he was shocked to learn that three days earlier his friend had hanged himself.

"Carl Messner was in excellent health and spirits when I heard from him last month," Haledjian told the sheriff. "I can't believe he committed suicide."

"He did — I investigated it myself," replied the sheriff. "Here's all there is to the case.

"Archie Carter, Mr. Messner's manservant, was returning to the house late that night when he noticed a light in the attic. As Carter got out of his car, he saw through the open attic window Mr. Messner knotting a rope around his neck. The other end of the rope was tied to a rafter. Then Mr. Messner calmly kicked away the small stool he was standing on, and that was it.

"Carter found the house doors locked. He had

forgotten his key so he ran to a neighbor and telephoned me. He reported to me exactly what I've
told you," said the sheriff.

"When I got out to the Messner house, I had to
force the front door. Then Carter and I dashed up
three floors to the attic. Mr. Messner was dead. The
coroner has no doubt death was from hanging.

"The attic floor was clear except for the little stool
that lay overturned by the door, and a broken clay
jug that must have been hit by the stool," concluded
the sheriff.

"I'd like to go out to the house again," said Haledjian. "From what you've told me of Carter's story,
he's lying!"

How did Haledjian know?

Archie Carter claimed he saw Carl Messner kick
a small stool from under him. However, standing on
the ground, Carter could never have seen a small
stool through an attic window three stories above
him!

6

The Case of the
Balloon Man

"The whole force is looking for Izzy the Balloon Man who kidnapped little Dennis Farrell," Inspector Winters said to Dr. Haledjian.

"Doesn't anyone know where Izzy hangs out?"

"Nobody knows anything about him," replied the inspector. "Once a week he stops his old truck by the Farrell estate and gives out popcorn and mouse-shaped pink balloons. The kids love the funny faces he makes as he puts the balloons to his lips and huffs and puffs.

"Last Thursday Izzy made his usual stop and drove off — or so it appeared. Later, Sam Potts and the Reverend Bevin were in Sam's backyard, which abuts the Farrell property. Sam noticed one of Izzy's balloons stuck high in his oak tree.

"Since there was no wind to blow it loose, Sam got a long ladder and climbed into the tree. From that height — about twenty feet — he could see over the Farrell's twelve-foot wall.

"Sam says that as he released the balloon he glanced into the Farrell yard and saw the Balloon Man put young Dennis into his truck and drive off. He told the minister what he'd seen. Neither man thought much of it till they heard that Dennis was missing.

"Yesterday," concluded the inspector, "Dennis's father received a note stating that Dennis was being held for ransom, and that instructions would follow."

"Putting together everything you've told me," said Haledjian, "I think both Dennis and the Balloon Man have been kidnapped!"

Why?

Haledjian realized Sam Potts had used the innocent clergyman to confirm a tale of kidnapping which never occurred as he reported it.

Potts had obviously stuck the balloon high in the oak as a prop. On a day without a wind, a balloon blown up by breath could never rise high into a tree.

The Case of the
Bamboo Fence

"Now this here place," said the bandy-legged little guide, "is Dead Man's Creek, being so named for the tragedy in '98."

Dr. Haledjian and the other dudes on the Wild West tour gazed blankly upon a muddy stream.

"Doc Holloway's cabin stood right there," continued the guide. "I guess Doc was the most popular fellow in these parts.

"Well, one afternoon Doc is patchin' up a peddler when Jim Sterling busts in. Jim says he was in town when a lone desperado with a pair of fancy six-shooters cleaned out the bank. In all the fuss and shootin', Jim is mistaken for the gunman and has to hightail it to save his hide.

" 'The bandit done dropped one of his sixes,' says Jim. 'Iffin I ever see the mate, I'll have me the real culprit.'

"There was no time for playin' detective just then.

9

A posse was comin'. Doc believed Jim was innocent, and so he puts on Jim's shirt and hat. Doc figures to lead the posse off long enough for Jim to escape.

"After getting his patient, the peddler, to keep his mouth shut, Doc cuts a length of rail about six feet long from his bamboo fence.

"He tells Jim to sit in the creek and breathe through the hollow bamboo, which is maybe as big around as a two-bit piece.

"Then Doc rides Jim's horse away, and the posse follows. Later, Jim is cleared, but it ain't no good. Jim is dead — drowned in the creek.

"The peddler fished him out an hour after Doc decoyed the posse. Doc reckoned poor Jim panicked underwater and drowned."

"He didn't panic," corrected Haledjian. "He was murdered."

How did Haledjian know?

Breathing through a tube six feet long and as big around as a two-bit piece (25¢), Jim would have passed out promptly. He would have been breathing in the same air as he had just expelled — air without oxygen — a simple medical fact Doc Holloway certainly knew!

The Case of the
Big Deal

Dr. Haledjian had just ordered a drink at the bar in the Las Vegas motel when a lean young stranger with sun-bleached golden hair and tanned cheeks took the stool beside him.

After asking for a gin and tonic, the sunburned young man nodded toward the gaming tables. "Name's Clive Vance," he said genially. "It's sure great to be back in civilization and hear money talking out loud."

The famous sleuth introduced himself. "I take it you've been out on the desert?"

"Got back yesterday," said Vance. "Washed the dust out of my ears, had a real live barber shave off seven months of whiskers and trim this mop of wheat. Then I bought a whole wardrobe on credit. All I had to show was my assay report. Boy, am I ever ready to celebrate."

"You found gold?"

"Right you are. Hit pay dirt." Vance stroked his bronzed chin thoughtfully. He lowered his voice confidentially.

"Listen," he said. "If I can find a backer, I'll take enough out of those hills to buy ten pleasure palaces like this one.

"Of course," he added apologetically, "I'm not trying to interest you, doctor. Still, if you know somebody who'd like to get in on a sure thing, let me know. I'm staying in room 210. Can't give out details here, you understand."

"I understand," said Haledjian, "that you'd better improve your story if you want to part some sucker from his money."

What was wrong with Vance's story?

Vance claimed he had a barber shave off "seven months of whiskers" the day before. Yet his cheeks were "tanned" and his chin was "bronzed." Had he really been in the sun seven months without a shave, his skin would have shown white where his whiskers grew.

The Case of the
Bitter Drink

Notwithstanding the 110-degree heat, the fifty American tourists seemed to have arrived in the Mexican village at a lucky time.

The initiation of a village youth to manhood was under way, the tour's guide announced.

A young man came jogging into the village. Sweating profusely, he sat down under a shade tree. Another villager fed him ice, wiped him dry, and massaged his neck and shoulders.

The tour's guide took a wooden cup from the local elder.

"Now comes the final test," said the guide. "The youth, having just completed a forty-mile run, must drink this cup of bitterest potion without changing expression."

The guide offered the cup to the tourists. Three men sipped it, and instantly gagged violently.

The guide talked quickly, and soon the Americans

13

were making large wagers with him that the youth could not pass the drinking test.

Dr. Haledjian, one of the tourists, never took his gaze from the cup, which passed to the youth undisturbed.

The youth drained it without batting an eye.

"You and the villagers have a neat con game here," Haledjian told the guide. "But I advise you to refund all bets, or I shall notify the district police!"

How were the tourists cheated?

The taste buds of the youth's tongue had been anesthetized by the ice fed him.

The Case of the
Blackmailer

"I don't mind telling you, Dr. Haledjian," said Thomas Hunt, "that inheriting the Hunt millions has had its nerve-racking moments. Do you remember Martin, the gardener?"

"A smiling and bowing little chap," said Haledjian, pouring his young friend a brandy.

"That's the fellow. I dismissed him upon inheriting the house in East Hampton. Well, three days ago he came to my office, bowing and smirking, and demanded one hundred thousand dollars.

"He claimed to have been tending the spruce trees outside my father's study when Dad drew up another will, naming his brother in New Zealand sole heir."

"You believed him?"

"I confess the news hit me like a thunderbolt. Dad and I had quarreled over Veronica sometime during the last week in November. Dad opposed the marriage, and it seemed plausible that he had cut me off.

"Martin asserted he possessed this second will, which he felt sure would be worth a good deal more to me than he was asking. As it was dated November 31 — the day after the executed will — it would be legally recognized, he claimed.

"I refused to be blackmailed. He tried to bargain, asking fifty thousand and then twenty-five thousand."

"You paid nothing, I hope?" asked Haledjian.

"I paid — with my foot firm on the seat of his pants."

"Quite right," approved Haledjian. "Imagine trying to peddle a tale like that!"

What was Martin's blunder?

No legal will could be dated November 31. November contains only thirty days.

The Case of the
Bogus Robbery

Since she was the richest woman in New York City, Mrs. Sydney had gratified every whim but one. She had never confounded Dr. Haledjian.

So Haledjian knew that the game of stump-the-detective had commenced again when at two o'clock in the morning he was summoned from the guest room of Mrs. Sydney's Fifth Avenue mansion by the butler who announced, "Madam's jewels have been stolen."

Entering Mrs. Sydney's bedroom, the famed sleuth closed the door and swiftly surveyed the scene.

The French windows were open. To the left of the disordered bed stood an end table with a book and two candles. The candles had burned down to three inches, spilling all their drippings down the side facing the door.

A bell cord lay on the thick green carpet. A drawer of the vanity table was open.

"What happened?" inquired Haledjian.

"I was reading in bed by candlelight when the door blew open," said Mrs. Sydney. "As you perhaps felt, a strong draft comes in. I pulled the bell cord for James, the butler, to come shut the door.

"Before he arrived, a masked man with a gun entered and forced me to tell him where I kept my jewels. As he scooped them into his pocket, James entered. The thief bound him with the bell cord and tied my hands and legs with these," she said, holding up a pair of stockings.

"As he departed, I asked him to have the decency to close the door. He merely laughed and deliberately left it open.

"It took James twenty minutes to work free and release me. I shall have a beastly cold in the morning!" concluded Mrs. Sydney.

"My compliments," said Haledjian, "on a nicely staged crime, with the fallacy fairly displayed."

What was the fallacy?

The candles spilled "all their drippings down the side facing the door."

Had the door really been left open as long as claimed, some wax would have dripped on the opposite side, away from the draft.

The Case of the
Broken Arm

"A knowledge of human behavior is often the explanation behind the criminologist's seemingly fantastic deductions," said Dr. Haledjian.

"A case in point was the murder of Roger Duffy, faked to look like suicide," said Haledjian. "Want to hear about it?"

"Can't we order dinner first?" said Octavia.

Haledjian smiled indulgently and continued.

"Duffy's body was found at 8 P.M. slumped on a park bench, a bullet in his left temple. His right arm, encased in a cast from fingertips to elbow since an accident the month before, lay on his lap. His left hand clutched a .32 pistol.

"Called to the scene and estimating that death had occurred about 7 P.M., I deduced from the contents of his pockets that he had been murdered in his bathroom and transported to the park.

"Astonishing, you gasp? Not at all. Since I real-

19

ized Duffy's clothes had been put on after his death, it seemed logical that he was undressed at the time of death. The hour pointed to an evening bath. Traces of blood in his bathroom confirmed my theory.

"Now, you ask, what was in his pockets that proved murder, not suicide? His right trouser pocket held four dollar bills clipped together and fifty-two cents in coins; his left trouser pocket had a handkerchief and cigarette lighter; his left hip pocket held his wallet.

"Surely you can see where the murderer made his mistake!" concluded Haledjian.

"Yes, killing Duffy on an empty stomach," said Octavia, filling up on water. "Who can think clearly when he's hungry? I give up."

Do you?

From the contents of Duffy's right-hand trouser pocket, Haledjian realized Duffy had not dressed himself.

With his right arm "encased in a cast from fingertips to elbow," he could not have fished into his right-hand trouser pocket. His right-side pocket would have been empty instead of containing commonly used articles such as money.

The Case of the
Bronze Nymph

"All the lights were out in the house last night when I heard a scuffling. I jumped out of bed to investigate and saw someone dash from my wife's room and race downstairs," Russell Evren told Inspector Winters.

"I gave chase. The intruder ran onto the back porch, where we keep a yellow insect light burning all night, and I recognized Jim Simmons."

"That's a lie!" shouted Simmons.

"Jim ran about a hundred yards," continued Evren, unruffled. "Then he threw something away. It struck several times on the rocky slope to the ravine, tracing its path in the darkness with a series of little sparks."

"Unfortunately for you, Mr. Simmons," said the inspector, "Mr. Evren was able to lead us right to the spot after he discovered his wife dead, and we found this."

The inspector held up a bronze statuette of a nymph. "Another hour and the hard rain that fell might have washed away all clues. The blood and hair found on the base match Mrs. Evren's. The lab got one good print — your forefinger."

"I wasn't near their house," protested Simmons. "Evren telephoned me early in the evening and told me he wanted to speak with me at my apartment at eight o'clock. He never showed. I stayed there until midnight, went out for a beer, and then hit the sack. As for the fingerprints, why, I handled that statuette while visiting the Evrens two days ago!"

That night the inspector told Dr. Haledjian, "Evren and Simmons are business partners who don't get along."

"Neither does Evren's attempt to frame Simmons," replied Haledjian.

Why not?

Evren claimed the "something" thrown by Simmons, which turned out to be a bronze nymph, the alleged murder weapon, struck sparks on the rocky slope, marking its path. Impossible.

Bronze, an anti-friction metal widely used in olden days for cannon, cannot strike sparks on rock.

The Case of the
Bumped Head

The express train running between New York and Los Angeles had to back up outside Chicago.

Alas, the engineer stopped the train too suddenly while in reverse. Passengers tumbled like tenpins, incurring several suits against the railroad.

"The stop happened at 9 P.M.," said Mills, the railroad's insurance man, while discussing the incident with Dr. Haledjian.

Mills related the biggest headache — Ted Sheldon, a passenger who was suing for one hundred thousand dollars.

"At 8 P.M.," said Mills, "Sheldon had the porter make up his berth in the last car. He claims he had just retired for the night when the stop occurred.

"He says he was so forcefully jerked that his head struck the wall behind his pillows.

"Because of terrific head pains, he says, he left the train at Chicago," concluded Mills. He showed

Haledjian a Chicago doctor's affidavit that Sheldon had suffered a skull fracture.

"You think Sheldon hurt his head somewhere else?" asked the sleuth.

"If I can't disprove his story about his hitting his head in the Pullman berth, the company is going to have to settle."

"You won't have any trouble," said Haledjian. *Why not?*

As all Pullman berths are made up with the head toward the front of the train, Sheldon, jerked by a train stopping while moving backward, would have banged his feet, not his head!

The Case of the
Buried Treasure

"From the gleam in your eye, I deduce you are about to get rich quick," said Dr. Haledjian.

"Clever of you, old chap," said Bertie Tilford, a young Englishman with a superiority complex toward work. "If I had a mere ten thousand I should realize a fortune! Have you ten?"

"What's the game now?" demanded Haledjian. "Pieces of eight among the corals? Doubloons from Kidd's chest?"

Bertie opened a sack and triumphantly produced a shining silver candlestick. "Sterling silver," he sang. "See what's engraved on the bottom."

Haledjian upended the candlestick and read the name *Lady North*. "Wasn't that the ship that sank in 1956?"

"The *Lady North* sank, but not with all hands as is generally believed," replied Bertie. "Four men

25

got away with a fortune in loot before the ship capsized in the storm.

"They hid their loot in a cave," continued Bertie. "But the storm started an avalanche and sealed off the entrance, burying three of the sailors inside. The fourth, a chap named Pembroot, escaped. Pembroot's been trying to raise ten thousand to buy the land on which the cave is located."

"You put up the money, the cave is opened, and the loot is divided two ways instead of four. Enchanting," said Haledjian. "Only how do you know Pembroot isn't a swindler?"

"Earlier tonight he took me to the cave," said Bertie. "This sack was half buried in the bushes, and I nearly sprained my ankle on it. I took one look and brought the candlestick here nonstop. You've got to agree it's the real thing, old chap."

"It is," admitted Haledjian. "And there's no doubt that Pembroot planted it by the cave for your benefit."

How did Haledjian know?

If the sterling silver candlestick had been lying in a sack since 1956, it would have been tarnished, not "shining."

The Case of the
Cave Paintings

"By Jove! This time I'm going to make us both rich!" exclaimed Bertie Tilford, the unemployed Englishman with more get-quick-rich schemes than tail feathers on a turkey farm.

He paused dramatically, eyeing Dr. Haledjian.

"You've heard of the caveman paintings in the Cave of Font de Gaume, France?" he resumed. "Well, my associate, Sebastian Delsolo, has found the greatest ever example of prehistoric art in a cave on a farm in Spain.

"Of course," went on Bertie, "I can't divulge the exact location yet. But we can buy the farm with the cave for a mite, dear boy. The farmer suspects nothing. Think of the fortune from tourists!"

Bertie passed three photos to Haledjian. "Behold! Sebastian pushed past subterranean water channels as far down as four thousand feet to photograph those drawings!"

27

The first photo was of a drawing of a woolly rhinoceros, the second of hunters attacking a dinosaur, the third of a charging mammoth.

"The cave artist worked by light from a stone lamp filled with fat and fitted with a wick of moss," explained Bertie. "He used pieces of red and yellow ochre for drawing and ground them and mixed them with animal fat for painting."

"How much to buy the farm?" asked Haledjian darkly.

"In American — fifty thousand dollars," said Bertie. "But you can have a third share of everything for a mere ten thousand."

"A third of nothing, you mean," corrected Haledjian. "I won't give you a nickel!"

Why not?

The drawing of "hunters attacking a dinosaur" was obviously a fake.

Man did not appear till millions of years after the dinosaurs had died out, and probably did not even suspect their existence.

The Case of the
Dead Boxer

Tony Cerone's worldly possessions were laid out on a small table in police headquarters. They consisted of a T-shirt, sneakers, and white cotton trousers. In a pocket of the trousers was a card.

The card read: July 28. Your wght, 173 lbs.; Your fortune, You will enjoy a long life.

"His life lasted 22 years," Inspector Winters told Dr. Haledjian.

"Late last night," said the inspector, "we got a call to come to the carnival. Somebody had started up a Ferris wheel. We found a male corpse jackknifed over a strut. At first I thought the guy had been beaten to death — his face was so battered. Then I recognized Tony.

"Last night Tony fought Kirby Malone for the state middleweight title," he continued. "Tony took a pounding. We know he left the arena still pretty dazed. He must have come out to the carnival. He used to be a roustabout, and he knew his way around.

"It looks like he got here after closing," said the inspector, "used the scale, and then started up the big wheel. He took a ride and fell out. The medical examiner says he died instantly."

The famed criminologist contemplated Tony's possessions.

"He might have been killed elsewhere and hung on the strut," said Haledjian. "I heard rumors of a fix in the Malone fight.

"It looks to me like Tony refused to take a dive and the mob made him pay the full price. The killers apparently did a clumsy job. To avoid giving themselves away, they changed his clothes and staged the scene out at the Ferris wheel."

How did Haledjian know?

Tony could not have gained 13 pounds in a day. He fought on the night of his death for the state middleweight — 160 pounds — title. When found, he had on someone else's clothing, for the card in his pocket gave his body weight as an impossible "173 lbs."

30

The Case of the
Coin Collector

Death, Dr. Haledjian ascertained quickly, had been inflicted by a blunt instrument within the past half hour.

He carefully rolled the body of his old friend, Hugh Clark, on its back. Something glinted within the red carnation in Clark's lapel. Haledjian recognized the object instantly — a gold stater of Croesus — a rare coin.

The sleuth replaced the coin in the carnation, rolled the body to its original position lying face down on the floor, and thoughtfully regarded the pockets, which were all turned inside out.

He was examining the kitchen of the dead man's three-room bachelor apartment when Clark's nephew, Jim Mimms, entered.

"Uncle Hugh is lying dead in the living room! What happened, Dr. Haledjian?" cried the young man.

Haledjian handed Mimms an open canister of flour to hold while he picked out the one marked tea.

"Your uncle," he said to Mimms, "telephoned me this morning and asked me to come right over. He was planning to take a rare coin downtown for sale and wanted me along. Apparently somebody arrived first — I found the door open — and slugged your uncle to death. The killer searched the body but found nothing, because your uncle didn't put the coin in his pocket!"

Haledjian paused to set a kettle of water on the stove. "You might bring the coin to me. It's buried in the flower."

Young Mimms put down the canister he was holding and left the kitchen. In a moment he was back with the coin, taken from the carnation.

"How deeply are you mixed up in this murder?" snapped Haledjian.

How come?

Mimms proved he was involved by taking the coin from the carnation, which he couldn't see because the body was "lying face down on the floor." Had he been innocent, he would have assumed when Haledjian said the coin was "buried in the flower," that it was buried in the flour — in the canister of flour he was holding.

The Case of the
Dead Broker

The corpse of Winthrop Parida sat facing the ocean on the deserted northern end of the boardwalk at Leedo Beach, slumped to the right against the arm of the stone bench.

From the bullet wound in the center of the forehead dried blood descended in a solid line down the right side of the face, staining his white collar and blue-dotted gold tie.

"A trash collector discovered the body at eight this morning," Inspector Winters told Dr. Haledjian.

"Death occurred between midnight and two this morning," said Haledjian. He studied the pistol on the boardwalk. "You're convinced it's suicide?"

"Parida's been despondent over the recent failure of his brokerage firm," replied the inspector. "Last night he attended a party. Afterward, the whole group drove out here in several cars to eat hot dogs at Benny's.

"It turned cold and a windstorm arose that didn't let up till dawn. Around 11 P.M. Parida excused himself and went outdoors. His friends got worried about him, but after waiting till 1 A.M., they figured he had gone home alone in his car. So they all returned to the city about 2 A.M.

"This wasn't the first time Parida had moodily walked out of a party in the past few weeks," concluded the inspector. "But nobody suspected he'd ever take his own life."

"He didn't," said Haledjian.

How did Haledjian know?

Had Parida shot himself on the bench during the windstorm, the blood from the wound would not have "descended in a solid line" down his face. The wind would have smeared it over his face and spattered it on his clothing.

Hence, Haledjian knew he was killed somewhere else and the suicide faked.

The Case of the
Dead Frenchman

The body of Yves du Motier was found in the bedroom of the apartment belonging to Silas Howe, the coin collector.

Du Motier had been stabbed to death with a letter opener. The body lay four feet from the rumpled bed.

"Death occurred about 8:30 A.M., or half an hour before the body was discovered," Inspector Winters told Dr. Haledjian.

"I telephoned Silas Howe, who has been in Philadelphia attending a numismatics convention. He says that last month he brought du Motier, a French coin collector and an old friend, from France for an operation to restore du Motier's hearing.

"The way it looks, somebody used a skeleton key to get into Howe's apartment and tried to steal his rare coins. Du Motier must have awakened, seen the intruder, and in the struggle was slain. The safe where Howe keeps his coins was unopened. No coins are missing as far as we can tell."

"Who notified the police?" inquired Haledjian.

"James Wilkes, a neighbor in the apartment house. Wilkes was on his way to work when he saw Howe's door open, and hearing the alarm clock ringing, investigated. He found the Frenchman dead on the floor."

"When did Howe leave for Philadelphia, and who can verify his presence there?" asked Haledjian.

"He left three days ago," said the inspector. "We contacted his hotel manager, who swears Howe was in and out on each of the past three days. Say — I see what you're getting at!"

Whom did Haledjian suspect?

Wilkes — who claimed to have been attracted by the ringing of the alarm clock — a fatal slip, since du Motier, who was deaf, would not have set the alarm.

The Case of the
Dead Judge

"Who are you?" demanded Dr. Haledjian of the sallow stranger who answered the doorbell at Judge Casper's residence.

"I'm Bernard Mitchell, Judge Casper's new law clerk," was the blurted answer. "The judge just killed himself!"

The sallow man led Haledjian into the den. Judge Casper lay slumped across his desk. Gripped in his left hand was a .32 revolver. His right hand rested on the desk beside a note.

Dr. Haledjian read:

"Since giving Arthur Brennet a suspended sentence, I have been the target of a defaming whispering campaign. I do not have the strength to keep asserting that I was not bought off. Were I younger, I should fight this libel. But for that I do not possess enough strength."

Said Mitchell, "The judge had been under attack

37

since he let off Brennet, the influence peddler, so lightly last year. Somebody started rumors that he'd been bribed. The remarks were libelous, and I kept urging him to sue. But he said he was too old for a fight."

Haledjian completed his examination of the bullet wound. "He's been dead only a few minutes. Did you hear a shot?"

"Yes, I dashed in here and found him already dead."

"How long have you been the judge's law clerk?"

"Only a week."

"Well, you'd better come with me to the police," said Haledjian. "They'll want to hear your alibi."

Why did Haledjian suspect Mitchell?

Haledjian knew Mitchell wasn't a law clerk. He and the judge's suicide note misused an elementary legal term to describe the defaming rumors — "libel" (published statement) instead of the proper word, "slander" (spoken statement).

The Case of the
Dead Millionaire

"I see Willie Van Swelte just reached his twenty-first birthday," said Inspector Winters, looking up from his newspaper. "Tomorrow he gets the ten million his father left him."

"Didn't the old man commit suicide twenty years ago?" asked Dr. Haledjian.

"Yes," replied the inspector. "And there was always something that puzzled me about the case. Edgar Van Swelte shot himself below the heart. The bullet passed upward, piercing the heart all right. Death was instantaneous. But why did he aim like that — upward?

"Another thing — no suicide note. Nobody was in the house when he died. I've got a picture of the scene, though."

The inspector drew a manila folder from his files and picked out a glossy print. It showed Edgar Van Swelte dead. His body, seated in the kitchen, had

39

fallen across the kitchen table. His right hand, still clutching the gun, rested on the table close beside the back of his head.

"The cook discovered the body upon returning from the market," continued the inspector. "She claims she telephoned the police promptly. When our photographer snapped this, it was 1 A.M. Edgar had been dead approximately six hours."

Haledjian studied the twenty-year-old photograph. Then he inquired, "How tall was Edgar?"

"Five-feet-eight, but long-legged, so that when he sat down, he appeared much shorter," answered the inspector.

"Then I should say there can be no doubt that he was murdered," announced Haledjian.

How did Haledjian reach his conclusion?

Had Van Swelte shot himself "from below the heart" while seated, he must have held the gun close to his lap. Since death was "instantaneous," it would have been impossible for him, a short-bodied man, to have lifted the hand with the gun until it "rested on the table" after shooting himself.

40

The Case of the
Dead Professor

"I heard a shot as I was sorting the silverware," said Mrs. Grummand, the housekeeper. "When I entered the study, Professor Townsend was li — like that!"

Seated at his desk was Reingald Townsend, chairman of the English Department of Overton University.

Haledjian studied the position of the body, which had sagged against the left arm of the leather swivel chair. The bullet had entered the right temple. A .38 caliber, double-action 1875 Army revolver lay in Townsend's lap.

On the desk was a note apparently signed by Reingald Townsend. Haledjian read:

"After having spoken with Dinker this morning, I have decided not to delay. I do what I must. Not even you, dearest Kay, can know the bottomless despair of being compelled to retire. Too old! To fully understand, one must have taught thirty-five years, as I have. Ahead is nothing. Farewell, I love you."

"Who are Dinker and Kay?" inquired Haledjian.

"Dinker is Paul Dinkerton, president of the university," replied the housekeeper. "Kay is Mrs. Townsend. She was called out of town suddenly. She left about ten this morning."

"Who are Professor Townsend's heirs?"

Mrs. Grummond hesitated. "Why, it is generally believed that Mrs. Townsend and I will share equally."

"Even if Professor Townsend was murdered?"

Why did Haledjian reject suicide?

The suicide note was an obvious phony. The chairman of the English Department would never have committed two grammatical sins — a redundant phrase and a split infinitive.

He would have written, "Having spoken," instead of "After having spoken," and "To understand fully," instead of "To fully understand."

42

The Case of the
Death at Sunrise

Inspector Winters raised the tattered window shade, letting morning light into the dingy room of Nick the Nose.

In the courtyard four stories below, policemen were gathered around the shattered body of a young woman.

"Let's hear it again," the inspector said to Nick.

Nick, who hadn't sold one of his phony tips to the police in months, shifted nervously.

"About sunrise I'm sitting in this chair reading the racing form," began the greasy little informer. "I got the insomnia, see? Suddenly I hear scuffling, and I see Mrs. Clark. She lives right across the court on the fourth floor.

"Well, she's struggling with a man in a uniform. He gives her a shove toward the window, and whammy, out she goes!

"The first thing I think of is you — maybe you'll

43

figure it's suicide instead of murder. So I run down to the drugstore and telephone you. I stayed with the body till we came up here, just to keep everything like it was for you."

Nick licked his lips. "I seen the killer's face. I figure I can identify him or at least tell you what kind of uniform he had on. That ought to be worth something."

"It is — this!" growled the inspector, delivering his foot to the seat of Nick's pants.

"Quite the appropriate payment," commented Haledjian when he heard of Nick's latest attempt at a payday.

Why did Nick get the boot instead of cash?

The inspector surmised that Nick had discovered the body while entering the building and concocted the murder angle for a buck.

He couldn't have seen from the window of his room what he described. The shade was drawn, remember?

The Case of the
Death Plunge

While browsing in the Professional Photographers' Exhibition, Dr. Haledjian stopped to admire a striking photograph in the flashgun category entitled "Death Plunge."

The print showed a small girl touching a lighted match to a Christmas candle. Beside the candle stood a pile of gifts. The girl was blonde, pug-nosed, adorable.

But what made the photograph spellbinding was the second figure.

It was a woman, back to camera, falling past the picture window just behind the little girl.

The caption read:

"This remarkable shot was taken August 24 at 9:30 P.M. by Bertram Kennedy in his Brooklyn studio apartment. At the moment Mr. Kennedy took the picture, Mrs. Claire Gramelin was falling from the roof six stories above. Her body, stopped in midair, produced this startling backdrop for what was intended as the Christmas cover of *Family Times Magazine*. It is believed Mrs. Gramelin, who weighed only ninety pounds, lost her footing in the storm winds which reached forty miles an hour that night. She died upon striking the sidewalk."

Haledjian finished reading as a group of officials moved in his direction. One of the men held a blue ribbon. As he was about to pin it to "Death Plunge," Haledjian spoke up.

"I wouldn't do that," cautioned the famed sleuth. "Unless you want to award first prize to an obvious fake!"

How did Haledjian know?

The picture window was closed, or else the little girl could not have held a lighted match in winds of "forty miles an hour." Therefore, the body of the woman could not have been seen falling outside. Remember, the shot was snapped at night with a flashgun, making the room brighter than the outdoors; thus, the window would have acted as a mirror, reflecting the room rather than transmitting the figure of Mrs. Gramelin.

The Case of the
Dentist's Patient

Dr. Evelyn Williams, London-born New York dentist, was preparing to take a wax impression of the right lower teeth of his patient, Dorothy Hoover. Silently the door behind him opened. A gloved hand holding an automatic appeared.

Two shots sounded. Miss Hoover slumped over, dead.

"We've got a suspect," Inspector Winters told Dr. Haledjian at his office an hour afterward. "The elevator boy took a nervous man to the fifteenth floor — Dr. Williams has one of six offices on the floor — a few moments before the shooting. The description fits John 'Torpedo' Burton.

"Burton is out on parole," continued the inspector. "I had him picked up at his rooming house. As far as he knows, I want to question him about a minor parole infraction."

Burton was ushered in and angrily demanded, "What's this all about?"

"Ever hear of Dr. Evelyn Williams?" asked the inspector.

"No, why?"

"Dorothy Hoover was shot to death less than two hours ago as she sat in a chair in Dr. Williams' office."

"I been sleeping all afternoon."

"An elevator operator says he took a man answering your description to the fifteenth floor a moment before the shots."

"It wasn't me," snarled Burton. "I look like a lot of guys. I ain't been near a dentist's office since Sing Sing. This Williams, I bet he never saw me, so what can you prove?"

"Enough," snapped Dr. Haledjian, "to send you to the chair!"

What was the basis of Haledjian's remark?

The Case of
Flawless Phil

"I've caught a good many crooks, but I've never tried to catch one while posing as a used-car salesman," confessed Dr. Haledjian.

"We think one of the men who have been smuggling dope across the border will be around for that car," replied Sheriff Monahan.

He pointed to a 1984 gray sedan. "Last week we got a tip that dope was being smuggled in a car parked outside Priestly's Bar & Grill. We missed the smugglers, but got the car. Under the back seat we found a million dollars worth of pure heroin.

"We had to rip up the entire floor of the car to get the stuff," the sheriff went on. "Phil Barton, who runs this car lot as Phil's Flawless Finds, agreed to put the car on display. It's bait. We hope the smugglers will try to find out if the dope is still hidden in it."

Haledjian agreed to play the part of a salesman.

On the windshield he stuck a poster that announced: Phil's Flawless Special Today Only.

After a while a dark-haired man moved toward the sedan.

"May I help you?" inquired Haledjian, and began his sales pitch. The customer edged toward the sedan without ever getting nearer than six feet of it. He seemed only halfheartedly interested as he peered at the engine.

Haledjian stepped around to the driver's window. "The engine has only twelve thousand miles on it. The inside," he admitted, "is floorless."

"Is it?" said the man, and walked hurriedly away.

"He's one of the smugglers," shouted Haledjian. "Arrest him!"

How did Haledjian know?

The man was scared off because he thought Haledjian said the car was "floorless," which in fact Haledjian did say.

But as the man never got close enough to see the floor of the car, he would have assumed, had he not been floor-minded, that Haledjian had said "flawless," the slogan of the car lot.

50

The Case of the
Footprint

Half a mile from where the body of Art Sikes, a hunter, had been found stabbed to death, was a rudely constructed hut.

The occupant, an eccentric hermit who grubbed a meager living from the surrounding forest by hunting and fishing, was the only human being found within thirty miles of the murder.

He was taken into custody protesting his innocence.

The local police chief established the following facts as the "wild man" crouched miserably in his jail cell grunting, "No kill man."

(1) Sikes had been stabbed two days before, or about the time the heavy rains had stopped.

(2) Since then an unseasonable heat wave had gripped the area, baking the ground dry.

Hearing that Dr. Haledjian was nearby, the police

chief summoned the sleuth to show off his up-to-date, scientific police methods.

"This morning we got the big break," said the chief. "We found a perfect right shoe print in the clay near the scene of the crime.

"We took a plaster impression," continued the chief. "It's the exact size and shape of that crazy man's new shoe."

Haledjian obtained permission to examine the suspect's shoes.

"His shoes are new, all right," said Haledjian, "but of a kind sold by the hundreds to trappers and hunters. I'm afraid, chief, your plastic impression does more to prove him innocent than guilty."

How come?

To be the killer's, the footprint had to be made when the earth was wet, but the impression was taken after the earth had been baked dry. As earth contracts in drying, shrinking footprints up to half an inch, the fact that the undersized print (made when the ground was baked dry) fit the suspect's shoe perfectly proved it was not made by him.

The Case of
Freddie the Forger

"Somebody tipped Freddie the Forger," Inspector Winters told Dr. Haledjian. "Freddie cleared out of his hotel room an hour before we raided it."

The inspector handed Haledjian a cardboard onto which a torn sheet of paper showing dates and places had been pasted together.

"We found the pieces in Freddie's wastepaper basket," the inspector said. "So at least we know where he's going."

Haledjian read the penciled notes: Paris, Aug. 14 . . . Naples, Sept. 12 . . . Athens, Sept. 21 . . . London, Oct. 3 . . . Palestine, Oct. 15 . . . Moscow, Dec. 24.

"Looks like an itinerary," agreed Haledjian. "But is it Freddie's?"

"Toby Kirk, Freddie's New York girl, insists it's his writing. She said she was in his hotel and overheard him making a long distance telephone call.

"He talked to Paris and got a hotel reservation for August 15. She didn't overhear much, but she thinks he then made a plane reservation for a flight that left New York at 2 P.M., August 14.

"Freddie's a smart operator," continued the inspector. "He always dreams up a new disguise. Toby Kirk says when he was in New York he bought a ten-gallon hat.

"I put Diehl, my best man, on the case. Diehl leaves tonight for France. If Freddie shows up in Paris wearing a fez, Diehl will spot him and bring him back."

"Unfortunately," said Haledjian, "Diehl will be flying in the wrong direction to capture Freddie."

How come?

The fact that Freddie wrote down Palestine instead of Israel as a destination told Haledjian he planned a transcontinental flight, not a transatlantic one. The new ten-gallon hat pinpointed Texas. Paris, Naples, Athens, London, Palestine, and Moscow are all towns in the Lone Star state.

The Case of the
French Vineyard

The dinner at the mansion rented by Pierre Gibrault was superb.

While the roast was being served, Gibrault arose, deftly unscrewed the cork from a chilled bottle of red table wine, and poured a little into the glass of Dr. Haledjian.

Haledjian sipped and politely nodded approval.

As Gibrault poured for his other guests, Jim Morgan, seated by Haledjian, whispered, "What do you think?"

"About the wine?" said Haledjian. "It's excellent!"

"You know, of course, why we were invited?"

"I expect Gibrault needs money," replied the sleuth.

"He was in my office last week," said Morgan, "to get a list of people who might be interested in investing in a French vineyard.

"Gibrault claims to be a wine exporter from Bor-

deaux, but I haven't had time to check him out,"
continued Morgan. "He assured me the vineyard up
for sale has the richest soil in France. It produces
the very best grapes. He wants to make red sparkling Burgundy to sell in America at top prices."

"How much cash does he need in a hurry?" asked
Haledjian.

"The vineyard's owner wants the equivalent of a
million American dollars, and he wants it by Tuesday or no sale," said Morgan. "I put your name on
the guest list because I thought you might help me
get a quick appraisal of Gibrault."

"I have," replied Haledjian. "Don't invest a
penny!"

Why not?

Haledjian knew Gibrault was a confidence man,
not a wine expert from Bordeaux, because: (1) he
served chilled red wine opened at the table when
red table wine should be opened an hour before serving and kept at room temperature; (2) "the richest
soil" does not produce the best grapes for wine; (3)
the poorest, not the best, French grapes go into red
sparkling Burgundy.

The Case of the
Green Pen

Except for the ambulance attendants, Sheriff Monahan, and Dr. Haledjian there was nobody at the Meadowbrook Bowling Lanes, the only alleys in town, except a young woman sprawled by the front door with a knife in her back.

"The lanes closed at midnight," said the sheriff. "One of my men discovered the body at 4 A.M., and I called you right away."

"Dead about an hour," said Haledjian. "Who was she?"

"Roberta Layne," replied the sheriff. "She just married Theodore Layne, a merchant captain, before he sailed for Hawaii last week. They have a little house on Bleaker Street."

"Any suspects?"

"Charlie Barnett — maybe. Roberta jilted him for Ted."

Haledjian dropped a green fountain pen by the door. "Let's pay Mr. Barnett a visit."

The suspect lived in a room behind the gasoline station he owned.

Haledjian's first words were, "Do you know Roberta has been murdered?"

"No!" gasped Barnett.

"Well, that's enough for now," said Haledjian.

Then, as if in afterthought, he added, "I must have dropped my fountain pen by the front door of the lanes where we found the body. I'm due in the city in an hour. Mind getting the pen for me and leaving it with the sheriff this morning?"

Barnett looked uncertain. He shrugged. "Sure."

When he brought the pen to the sheriff's office later that morning he was promptly arrested.

Why?

Although Barnett claimed he did not know Roberta Layne had just been murdered, he knew, as Haledjian said, that the pen lay "by the front door of the lanes." Had he been innocent, he would have looked for the pen at the front door of the Laynes — that is, at their house.

The Case of the
Haunted House

"You can't rent more for your money than this house," said Tilford, the real estate agent. "It has charm, fancy brickwork, half-timbering, casement windows, three terraces, and a lady ghost."

"Ghost?" inquired Dr. Haledjian, pushing open a bedroom window. He gazed upon the flagstone terrace two stories below.

"The ghost is Jennifer Godley," explained Tilford. "This was her house. On March 28, 1979, she was hurled from this very window. Her body was found on the stones below.

"At first the police thought she was a suicide, or had accidentally fallen," continued Tilford. "They then realized that this window was closed when she was found.

"Henry Godley, her husband, admitted entering the bedroom and closing the window himself. It was a chilly day, and he claimed that he didn't know his wife lay dead on the stones below. Of course, he was sentenced to life — "

"Whoa!" cried Haledjian. "On what evidence?"

"Ben Taylor, a schoolteacher, saw the whole thing. He was out bird-watching. The Godleys lived like hermits — never had visitors, didn't allow anyone within a mile of the place. But Ben Taylor had binoculars, and at the trial he testified that he saw Henry Godley slide up the window and throw poor Jennifer head first to the terrace."

Haledjian pursed his lips in thought. The next day he telephoned Tilford.

"I've decided not to rent the house for the summer," he said. "But I'm going to see that Henry Godley is given a new trial!"

Why?

Ben Taylor lied in testifying he saw Godley "slide up" the window by which he allegedly threw his wife to her death.

It was a casement window, which is hinged, and which Haledjian opened by "pushing."

The Case of the
Hero Dog

"My pitch last night was beautiful," Cyril Makin, the woeful wooer, told Dr. Haledjian. "How did Trudy Shore ever see through it?

"For three generations," continued Makin, "Trudy's family have been circus people doing a dog act. If you aren't a canine connoisseur with a fabulous dog somewhere in the family, she won't date you twice. So to score with her, I made up a grandpa and his faithful four-legged helper."

Makin sipped his drink disconsolately. Then he recounted his latest unsuccessful pitch.

"Near Grandpa's farm the railroad tracks made a hairpin turn between two stony cliffs. From his fields, Grandpa could see the tracks. If rocks fell upon them, Grandpa climbed a hill and warned the engineer by waving a red flag.

"One day Grandpa saw rocks falling on the tracks. He started for the hill as a train approached, but

61

tripped and knocked himself unconscious. That's when the dog proved his mettle.

"The dog raced to the house. The dog pulled down Grandpa's long red underwear from the clothesline, raced to the hill, and there ran back and forth, trailing the red underwear like a warning flag.

"The engineer saw the red signal and stopped the train, saving hundreds of passengers from death or injury!" concluded Makin.

"You're lucky," said Haledjian, "Trudy didn't bite your nose off for a dog story like that!"

What was wrong with it?

Dogs are color-blind.
or that the underwear was red.
have known that the flag Grandpa waved was red,
Unfortunately for Cyril's pitch, the dog couldn't

The Case of the
Hidden Diamond

The thieves spent six hours in the home of Ted Duda.

At first they searched the house, trying to find where he hid his huge diamond, valued at half a million dollars.

Then they tried beating the information out of him. They fled at dawn, fearing detection.

Fatally hurt, Duda crawled to his desk and typed a note to his partner, John Madden.

It read:

"John — four men tried to make me tell where I had hidden the diamond. At first they looked through the house, raving like madmen. Then, in desperation, the barbarians split open the cat! When all failed, they beat me, but I did not tell. I'm dying. The diamond is hidden in the vane."

"Duda died this morning," Inspector Winters told

Dr. Haledjian. "We have his murderers, but not the diamond."

The inspector handed Haledjian a copy of the death note. "We took down the weathervane, a cock, but there wasn't anything inside it," the inspector said. "We're still searching the house."

Haledjian read the note and said, "You also failed to find the body of the cat, but you did find a broken barrel of liquor."

"Why, yes," said the inspector. "The thieves were thorough. They broke the barrel and every bottle in Duda's little wine cellar."

"How many walking sticks did Duda own?"

The inspector looked puzzled. "One."

"It must be hollow," said Haledjian. "You'll find the diamond inside it."

The inspector did. But how did Haledjian know?

Haledjian realized that the dying Duda could not have typed errorlessly, as it appeared. He quickly saw that Duda had interchanged the "v" and "c" which are positioned next to each other on the typewriter keyboard.

Reread the note, substituting the "v" for the "c," and vice versa.

The Case of the
Hitchhiker

"Boy, thanks for the lift," exclaimed the young man as he slid off his knapsack and climbed into the front seat of the air-conditioned patrol car beside Sheriff Monahan. "Say, aren't you going to arrest me for bumming a ride?"

"Not today," replied the sheriff. "Too busy."

The young man grinned in relief. He took a chocolate bar from his knapsack, broke off a piece, and offered the rest to the sheriff.

"No, thanks," said the police officer, accelerating the car.

"You chasing someone?" asked the hitchhiker.

"Four men just held up the First National Bank. They escaped in a big black sedan."

"Hey," gasped the hitchhiker. "I saw a black sedan about ten minutes ago. It had four men in it. They nearly ran me off the road. First car I saw in an hour. But they took a left turn. They're headed west, not north!"

Sheriff Monahan braked the patrol car and swung it around. The young man began peeling an orange, putting the rinds tidily into a paper bag.

"Look at the heat shining off the road ahead," said the sheriff. "Must be eighty-five in the shade today."

"Must be," agreed the hitchhiker. "Wait — you passed the turnoff — where're you going?"

"To the police station," snapped the sheriff — a decision to which Haledjian heartily agreed upon hearing the hitchhiker's story.

How come?

The hitchhiker quickly confessed to being one of the hold-up gang, left behind to misdirect pursuit. His story was obviously phony, since he "broke off a piece" of chocolate. Standing for more than an hour in eighty-five-degree heat, as he claimed, the chocolate bar would have been soupy.

The Case of the
Home Bakery

"I was driving by when I got the darndest attack of indigestion," said Sheriff Monahan apologetically. "Do you have some bicarbonate of soda?"

Mrs. Duffy, a motherly woman of sixty, smiled cheerfully. "You just sit right down in the kitchen, Sheriff," she said. "I don't keep bicarbonate of soda on hand, but I'll brew you a nice cup of tea. It'll work wonders, I promise."

Sheriff Monahan seated himself obediently while Mrs. Duffy bustled about her neat little kitchen. He had always admired the kindly woman who dwelt alone and made her own living.

After the sheriff had finished his tea, he rose to leave. "I feel better already. Many thanks."

Outside, he saw Mrs. Duffy's panel truck. It was parked by the south wing of the house which, he had always assumed, was her bakery, in which she

67

made the bread, cakes, and pies she sold to inns along the highway.

He studied the pink lettering on the truck: "Ma Duffy's Homemade Pies, Cakes, and Bread." He stared thoughtfully at the house.

Back in town he telephoned Dr. Haledjian. The famed criminologist heartily advised him to get a search warrant, and within the hour the sheriff had returned to Mrs. Duffy's.

A search of the premises disclosed that Ma Duffy's pies, cakes, and bread were commercial products with wrappers removed. But the bottles of whiskey illegally secreted within each pullman loaf were strictly home brewed.

What made the sheriff suspicious?

The sheriff realized that Mrs. Duffy wasn't baking in the back of her house when she said, "I don't keep bicarbonate of soda on hand." Bicarbonate of soda is another term for baking soda, which anyone doing baking would stock as a staple.

The Case of the
Hotel Murder

Dr. Haledjian was shaving in his hotel room on the second floor when he heard a woman screaming, "Help!"

Tossing on his robe, he dashed into the hall. In front of room 213 a woman stood crying and screaming.

Introducing himself, Haledjian looked through the open door and saw a man slumped in an easy chair. A swift examination showed he had just been killed by a bullet through the heart.

"Try to get hold of yourself and tell me what happened," said the sleuth.

"I'm Clara Uffner," sobbed the woman. "A few moments ago I heard a knock on the door. A voice said, 'Telegram.'

"I opened the door. A masked man stood there, a gun in his gloved hand. He shot my husband, tossed the gun into the room, and ran."

The automatic pistol on the floor, Haledjian saw, was equipped with a silencer. Returning to the hall, he noted the door at one end marked Exit.

Reentering the room, he stepped on something hard. It turned out to be an empty cartridge shell. Farther to the left was another. Both were of the caliber to match the pistol.

Embedded in the wall, about two feet above the seated body, Haledjian discovered a second bullet.

"All right, Mrs. Uffner," he said sternly. "Now tell me the truth!"

Why did he doubt Mrs. Uffner?

Had the mysterious killer fired from the hall into the room, the shells from his gun would not have fallen forward into the room and to the left. An automatic pistol ejects to the right and a few feet behind the shooter.

The Case of the
Hunting Accident

Dr. Haledjian's weekend hunting trip ended abruptly when he stumbled upon the body of a middle-aged man dressed in hunter's garb lying in a shallow gorge.

An autopsy disclosed that death had been instantaneous. A bullet had entered just above the hip and lodged in the heart.

Investigation by the police established the dead man as John C. Mills, a New York City ad man. Further, Mills and a friend, Whit Kearns, had rented a hunting lodge near where the body was found.

Kearns was immediately brought in for questioning.

A suave, impeccably tailored sportsman of fifty, Kearns looked from the inspector to Dr. Haledjian before saying resignedly, "All right. I didn't mean to run away. I suppose I just panicked.

"Johnny Mills and I rent the same lodge every year," continued Kearns. "We've never failed to bring back one bear at least.

"We had spent a week in the woods and our time was up. It was the last day, and for the first time we hadn't shot a solitary bruin. I noticed a rock formation and climbed to the top to see if I couldn't spot one.

"Suddenly I heard John shout in terror in the clearing below me. A bear had got to him. I shot, but only wounded the bear. It reared on its hind legs. Just as I fired again, John got in the way. My bullet struck him, and he tumbled into the gorge.

"The bear disappeared," concluded Kearns. "I panicked, I admit, but I swear it was an accident!"

"The facts," said Haledjian quietly, "disprove your tale."

What was Kearns' slip?

Shooting into "the clearing below" from atop a rock formation, Kearns' bullet would have followed a downward angle. But the bullet that killed Mills traveled upward — from hip to heart.

72

The Case of the
Indian Jug

The day before the big Tech vs. State football game, the State mascot, an Indian jug, disappeared.

Three hours before kickoff, one of the State fraternities was anonymously informed that the jug was buried on the estate of E. B. Van Snite, millionaire Tech grad, fanatical football booster, and notorious prankster.

Six State undergraduates enlisted the aid of Dr. Haledjian. Arming them with shovels, the famous sleuth drove out to see Van Snite, an old friend.

"Certainly the jug is buried here," Van Snite said, his eyes twinkling mischievously.

The State boys gazed with dismay upon the area of ground Van Snite had indicated.

It was a freshly turned half acre, scraped and rolled and freshly sown on every inch with grass seed.

The area was walled on three sides, and a stone

walk bordered the fourth. In dead center stood a bird bath. A maple tree grew at one end of the expanse and two wild olive trees at the opposite end.

"You have two hours till kickoff," said Van Snite. "The jug is hidden in the only reasonable place in the half acre.

"Find it, and you can have it back. But if you fail by game time, you must pay for planting the whole lawn."

The State boys prepared to leave. But within half an hour they had unearthed the Indian jug — after Haledjian had told them where to dig.

Where?

"The only reasonable place" was where Van Snite didn't expect to grow a lawn anyway.

That meant under the maple, whose surface roots steal food and moisture from the smaller grass roots, making grass impossible.

The Case of the
Indian Trader

Dr. Haledjian and the rest of the saddle-sore dudes on the deluxe tour of western sites entered the adobe museum and stared at an empty green-tinted glass bottle.

Its label read: Doc Henry's Secret Elixir.

The tour's bandy-legged little guide recounted the reason for the bottle's enshrinement.

"Beautiful Jinny Knox was saved by seventy-seven of them bottles back in '83," he began.

"Ol' Doc Henry was an Injun trader — never sold a drop of his elixir to a white man, only to them Injuns. 'Course, Doc kept the ingredients a secret. But on his deathbed, he's supposed to have admitted it weren't nothin' but sugar water.

"Well, one night some crazy drunk Injuns kidnaped young Jinny. It was Doc Henry who volunteered to go after her.

"He set off with a wagonload of tradin' goods and

eighty bottles of his elixir hung from the beams. For five days of sub-freezin' weather he palavered with them savages.

"But Doc brings Jinny home safe. He'd had to trade all his bottles but three fer her, and all his other stuff in the bargain.

"Doc," concluded the guide, "was a hero. Imagine goin' up into them hills alone and tradin' a pack of crazy-drunk redskins out of a beautiful girl!"

"Doc was no hero," corrected Haledjian. "He was an old rascal who was partly responsible for Jinny's kidnapping!"

How did Haledjian know?

After "five days of sub-freezin' weather" the "sugar water" would have frozen and broken the glass bottles. Hence the elixir had to be something with a low freezing point — an alcoholic beverage that got the Indians "crazy drunk."

The Case of the
Last Moreno

"From the smirk connecting your ears, I assume you've hit upon a new scheme for making a million dollars," Dr. Haledjian said to Bertie Tilford.

"Not quite a million," corrected Bertie, a young Englishman with more ways to avoid work than aces up the sleeve of a Mississippi gambler.

Bertie opened his briefcase and showed Haledjian a pen-and-ink sketch of a bearded man.

"Looks like a Tassado Moreno!" Haledjian marveled.

"Precisely," gloated Bertie. "All the world knows the great artist died in Alaska three years ago. The details were never divulged till his friend, Kiako, meeting hard times, came to me.

"The facts are," continued Bertie, "that Moreno injured his hip in a storm that buried his and Kiako's supplies on the trail. The weather had been far below freezing for days, and Moreno, his hip injured, failed rapidly.

"Kiako got him to an abandoned shack. He stopped up the broken window with his gloves. As he tore apart a chair to build a fire, Moreno called to him. There was no time. He wouldn't live half an hour.

"Moreno asked for drawing materials. Kiako found an old pen and a bottle of ink in a cupboard. Moreno sketched his faithful friend, and died.

"The prices of Morenos have soared since his death. His last picture should be worth a quarter of a million. I can buy it from Kiako for twenty thousand," concluded Bertie. "Have you twenty, old boy?"

"For that portrait? Not twenty cents!" snapped Haledjian.

Why not?

As "the weather had been far below freezing for days," and the shack had a "broken window," the ink would have been frozen solid and impossible to draw with.

The Case of the
Lazy Murderer

According to the coroner's report, Mrs. Treddor, the town recluse, had been bludgeoned to death two days ago in the kitchen of her decaying hilltop mansion.

"I received an anonymous telephone call at 4 A.M. yesterday that she had been murdered," Sheriff Monahan confessed to Dr. Haledjian. "Heaven help me, I thought it was just another prank and didn't investigate till this afternoon!

"Living alone, never showing herself anywhere, why Mrs. Treddor's been the butt of every practical joke in the book, including the death gimmick, a dozen times."

The sheriff conducted Haledjian onto the front porch. "It got so no store in town would send anything on a telephone order. Had to have it in writing. Aside from a daily milk and newspaper delivery, the only visitors who climbed up to see her regularly were the weekly grocery boy and Doc Bentley, both due tomorrow. You can see why."

Haledjian gazed down a long slope of underbrush to the road below. The driveway to the house was overgrown and impassable, and deliveries obviously had to be made on foot.

The famed sleuth sat down in a rocking chair, the only object on the sagging porch besides two unopened newspapers.

"Who was the last person to see Mrs. Treddor alive?"

"Mrs. Carson, probably," said the sheriff. "Early on the day of Mrs. Treddor's death, she was driving by and noticed the old lady come out on the porch to take in her bottle of milk."

The sheriff paused. "Mrs. Treddor was supposed to have fifty thousand dollars hidden someplace. We can't find it, or any clues."

"Except for that anonymous telephone call," corrected Haledjian. "The murderer never figured you wouldn't investigate within the hour!"

Whom did Haledjian suspect?

The milkman, who thought he didn't have to make his daily delivery. There were two newspapers on the porch, but no bottles of milk.

80

The Case of the
Locked Room

"I think I've been taken for ten thousand dollars, but I can't figure out how it was done," said Archer Skeat, the blind violinist, to Dr. Haledjian, as the two friends sat in the musician's library.

"Last night Marty Scopes dropped by," continued Skeat. "Marty had a ginger ale — and we got to chatting about the locked room mysteries till I made this crazy ten-thousand-dollar bet.

"Marty then went to the bar over there, filled a glass with six cubes of ice and gave it to me. He took a bottle of ginger ale and left the room.

"I locked the door and the windows from the inside, felt to make sure that Marty's glass held only ice, and put it into the wall safe behind you. Then I turned off the lights and sat down to wait.

"The bet was that within an hour Marty could enter the dark, locked room, open the locked safe, take out the glass, remove the ice, pour in half a glass of ginger ale, lock the safe, and leave the room, locking it behind him — all without my hearing him!

"When the alarm rang after an hour, I had heard nothing. Confidently, I unlocked the door. I kept Marty whistling in the hall when I crossed the room to the opposite wall and opened the safe. The glass was inside. By heavens, it was half filled with ginger ale and only ginger ale. I tasted it! How did he do it?"

"Undoubtedly by means of an insulated bag," replied Haledjian after a moment's thought. "There is nothing wrong with your hearing. But no man could have heard — "

Heard what?

Ice melting. Marty had brought him with him frozen cubes of ginger ale. After setting up the bet, he had slipped the ginger ale cubes into the glass. While they melted in the glass inside the safe, Marty waited in the hall!

The Case of the
Lookout

Dr. Haledjian was the only customer in the little drugstore when the shooting started.

He had just taken his first sip of black coffee when three men dashed from the bank across the street, guns blazing.

As the holdup men jumped into a waiting car, a nun and a chauffeur sought refuge in the drugstore.

"You're both upset," said Haledjian. "Let me buy you a cup of coffee."

They thanked him. The nun ordered black coffee, the chauffeur a glass of root beer.

The three fell to talking about the flying bullets and had barely touched their drinks when sirens sounded.

The robbers had been captured and were being returned to the bank for identification.

Haledjian moved to a front window to watch. As

he returned to the counter, the nun and chauffeur thanked him again and departed.

The counterman had cleared the glass and cups. "Sorry, mister," he said to Haledjian. "I didn't know you weren't done."

The counterman looked at the two coffee cups he had just removed from the counter, and passing Haledjian the one without lipstick, said, "What do you think a chauffeur was doing around here? There isn't a limousine on the street."

Haledjian thought a moment. "Good grief!" he cried. "We had the gang's lookout right here!"

And he dashed out to make the capture.

What aroused Haledjian's suspicion?

The woman dressed as a nun admitted being the lookout after Haledjian had seized her down the block.

Haledjian, too, had noticed the lipstick on her coffee cup and knew she was not a real nun, since nuns don't wear lipstick.

84

The Case of the
Lost City

"I'm really onto something big this time," said Bertie Tilford, the irrepressible Englishman with more get-rich-quick schemes than horsehair in a mattress factory.

He fished a letter from his pocket and pressed it to Dr. Haledjian. "Run your eyes on this, old boy!"

The letter, addressed to Bertie, was signed "Baron Stramm." Haledjian read:

"Am positive I have located the lost city of Heliopaulis which was buried by the eruption of Mount Vitras in 147 A.D. Can you rush me thirty thousand dollars to begin excavations?"

"Baron Stramm," explained Bertie, "came to see me before departing on his search for Heliopaulis last year. He said if he ever found the city, he'd let me in on the ground floor, so to speak. A half share of everything — if I backed him."

Bertie grinned smugly. "Can you imagine what a

discovery like Heliopaulis will be worth?"

"Of course," said Haledjian. "You'd like to raise some of the thirty thousand from me?"

"A pittance, my dear chap. A mere bagatelle," said Bertie. "I'm doing you a favor. Let me have ten thousand and I'll make your fortune!"

"I don't know anything about your Baron Stramm," said Haledjian, "or the lost city of Heliopaulis. But the man who wrote that letter is obviously not an archaeologist. So no money today for your swindler, my boy!"

Why not?

A bona fide archaeologist would never have written "in 147 A.D." A.D. means "anno Domini" (in the year of the Lord) and, unlike B.C., always precedes the date; as, A.D. 147.

The Case of the
Maestro's Choice

Even by the night of the concert, Gregory Pitz, the famous conductor, hadn't decided which of his star pupils, Ivan Poser or Mark Donn, would make his violin debut.

The anxious youths dressed in separate private dressing rooms. Fifteen minutes before curtain time, Pitz made up his mind.

He told Poser he had been selected; then he broke the sad news to Donn.

Ten minutes later Pitz went to fetch Poser for the performance. The youth lay dead in the middle of the tiny dressing room floor, shot through the head.

Trembling, Pitz locked the door and summoned his old friend, Dr. Haledjian, from the wings.

Haledjian urged the maestro to play the concert and followed him into Donn's dressing room.

Hearing that he was to perform after all — without hearing why — Donn looked surprised and pleased. He straightened his tie, picked up his violin and bow, and followed Pitz downstairs and onto the stage.

The two musicians bowed to the applause. Donn waited stiffly till Pitz signaled the orchestra. Then the youth raised his violin to his chin.

A moment later Donn was stroking the opening notes. Haledjian telephoned the police and advised them to arrest the young violinist.

Why?

The fact that Donn was prepared to perform and therefore was aware of Poser's death indicated he was involved in the murder.

Had he been unaware, he would have stopped to rosin his bow and tune his violin before playing.

The Case of the
Missing Button

Matty Linden, a husky tenth-grade student, scowled at Inspector Winters. "You must be some kind of nut. I didn't slug Miss Casey, and I didn't steal her purse!"

"No? Unfortunately for you, a ninth-grade girl happened to enter the corridor where Miss Casey lay. The girl saw a boy in a dark cardigan sweater and brown pants leaving by the door at the far end."

The inspector paused and then demanded, "Do you always wear your sweater buttoned?"

"Sure," replied Matty. "Why?"

"Because you might have noticed the third button from the top is missing," snapped the inspector. He held up the missing button. "The girl who spotted you found the button clasped in Miss Casey's hand."

"I lost that button two days ago," retorted Matty. "This girl — how could she be sure it was me in that long corridor?"

"She isn't positive — she saw only your back. But this missing button proves you did it. Luckily, Miss Casey isn't badly hurt. Now, where's her purse?"

"Matty kept insisting he didn't know a thing about the slugging and theft," the inspector told Dr. Haledjian later.

"No doubt," said Haledjian, "the boy had some silly alibi about where he was when Miss Casey was slugged and robbed?"

"Right. He claims he got a note to be in the school boiler room at ten — fifteen minutes before Miss Casey was assaulted. He waited half an hour, but nobody showed up."

"I trust you made an arrest?" asked Haledjian. *What was the guilty student's error?*

In trying to frame Matty Linden, the ninth-grade girl made too much of a point of the cardigan, which he always wore buttoned. Since she saw only the back of a boy leaving the corridor, she could not have known whether his sweater was a pullover or a cardigan unless she knew beforehand, having stolen the button from it.

The Case of
Molly's Mule

Cyril Makin, the amateur amorist, sagged dejectedly into a chair in Dr. Haledjian's home. "I got slapped last night," he moaned. "I can't figure what was wrong with my pitch this time.

"I was trying to impress Libby McMurdoch," continued Cyril. "You know her — her father owns Greenpoint Farms, the big racing stable.

"Animals come before anything in the McMurdoch book. Why last year her old man scratched his ace thoroughbred from the Garden Classic because he suspected a sore hoof. Gave up a crack at a hundred thousand dollars!

"Well, I had to top that animal-before-money bit," Cyril continued. "So I unbottled my great-uncle, Death Valley Tim, and his faithful mule Molly M. I told Libby about how Uncle Tim and Molly M went into the desert in '89. That trip Uncle Tim hit the mother lode, richest gold strike ever. But did he haul it right away? No, sir! Molly M was ailing, and Molly M came before anything.

"Uncle Tim just waited, week after week. Finally Molly M had her little one, Strike-It-Rich, but Uncle Tim waited another week till Molly M was strong enough to tote a load of gold.

"When Tim returned to the desert, he discovered a storm had wiped out all trace of the diggings. He never found the spot again. Five or six million were lost by waiting for Molly M instead of making two or three quick trips, though the poor beast wasn't fit for heavy work."

"About there," broke in Haledjian, "Miss Libby McMurdoch, the animal-lover, decided that you weren't fit for her!"

Why not?

No mule — not even Molly M — can reproduce.

The Case of
Murder at the Zoo

The headlights of Dr. Haledjian's car flooded over a blond man darting across the road. Haledjian spun the steering wheel and slammed on the brakes. "Are you all right?" he called anxiously.

"I'm okay," the man gasped. "But there's somebody — I think he's dead — lying in the zoo. I was running to get the police."

Explaining he was a doctor, Haledjian persuaded the blond man to show him the corpse. About a hundred yards from the road, near the giraffe enclosure, lay a figure in a doorman's uniform.

"He's just been slain," said Haledjian. "Shot in the back. Do you know him?"

"No," the man said. "My name is Chris Taylor. I was out for a walk when a car passed me a few minutes ago. It was traveling very slowly.

"The next thing I knew, an orange flame appeared in the back of the car. Then a giraffe began to scream as if in pain. The enclosure is visible from the road, and I saw one giraffe running in circles and suddenly collapse. I went to investigate and stumbled on the body here."

"I want to see the giraffe," muttered Haledjian. He climbed the fence and knelt beside the stricken animal. "Poor creature has been shot in the neck."

"The way I figure it," said Taylor, "the killer must have missed his man and hit the giraffe with his first shot. The second bullet found the mark, though."

"Undoubtedly that is what happened," agreed Haledjian. "Except for one thing. You weren't running to get help. You were running away!"

How did Haledjian know?

Taylor claimed that he stumbled on the dead man after being attracted by the "scream" of the giraffe. Unfortunately for his story, a giraffe is voiceless.

The Case of
Murder Before the Concert

The body of pretty Frieda Dillon lay beside her green sedan in the driveway of the boardinghouse where she had lived. She had been slain at 8 P.M., some fifteen minutes before she was due at the Civic Auditorium to perform in a concert slated for 8:30 P.M.

She had been shot twice. The first bullet had pierced her right thigh, leaving a large bloodstain on her dark sheath skirt. The second and fatal bullet had pierced her heart, leaving a bloodstain on her white blouse.

Inside the sedan was Miss Dillon's cello.

The police took testimony from three persons.

The landlady, Mrs. Wilson, who found the body, said Frieda had decided to attend the concert but not to play, because she had been annoyed by an over-ardent suitor, Bill Sanders, a fellow orchestra member. Frieda hadn't practiced her cello or taken it from the car in a week.

Bill Sanders insisted that he and Frieda had patched up their romance. She had told him she would play, and that she'd pick him up at 8:10 P.M. and they would drive together to the auditorium as they always did. But he had waited for her in vain.

Lazlo St. John, the conductor, said that the women members of the orchestra wore dark skirts and white blouses, and the men wore white jackets and black trousers, though minor details of style were optional. The orchestra members dressed at home. He added that Frieda undoubtedly could perform well without any practice, since the concert was a repeat program.

After reading the three statements, Haledjian immediately knew Sanders was lying.

How?

Haledjian knew that Frieda Dillon had no intention of playing with the orchestra, as Bill Sanders claimed. She was a cellist, and could not possibly have performed wearing a sheath skirt.

The Case of the
Murdered Camper

Dr. Haledjian and Sheriff Monahan had scarcely finished supper when Wyatt Fulton burst into their camp clearing.

"Hurry, Sheriff," he cried. "Bob's been killed!"

During the five-minute tramp to his campsite, Fulton recounted what had happened.

"An hour ago, just as Bob and I were going to have coffee, two men with rifles stepped out of the woods. We mistook them for hunters till they announced a holdup.

"Bob jumped one, but the other struck him on the head with a rock. They tied us up and stole our money.

"I finally worked free and cut Bob loose — he was dead. I remembered you'd gone camping, Sheriff. So I looked for your fire."

At Fulton's campsite, Haledjian's practiced eye missed nothing.

Bob Swamm's body lay on its back near the fire. Near the body were several strands of rope and a bloody rock. A yard away was the uncut rope that had apparently been used to bind Fulton.

Two sleeping bags and two knapsacks lay on the ground. On a large flat stone were pairs of plates, forks, cups, and knives. The cups were unused.

"Bob Swamm died about an hour ago, probably from the blow on the head," Haledjian said.

For a moment afterward the only sound in the clearing was the hissing from the fire as the small black coffee pot cast boiling drops over the brim and onto the flaming logs below.

Haledjian broke the silence. "A neatly staged murder scene, Fulton. But you made one fatal mistake."

What was the mistake?

Had the coffee pot been put on the fire before the two holdup men murdered Swamm, "an hour ago," as Fulton claimed, the water would have boiled away far below the brim of the small pot.

Hence Fulton had just put on the pot before running to fetch the sheriff.

The Case of the
Murdered Skier

When a mid-January thaw melted the snowdrifts in the Adirondack Mountains, a late-model sports car was found parked on a side road near the Guilden Ski Lodge. Inside were the bodies of May Elliot and Roger Kirk, victims of rifle shots. Both had registered at the resort a week earlier under fictitious names.

"We checked out Miss Elliot — nothing," said Inspector Winters to Dr. Haledjian as the two men stood in the trophy-hung living room of Roger Kirk.

Haledjian read a maple plaque awarded to Kirk as runner-up in the 1979 World Water Ski championships.

Then he moved to a table whereon were four birthday gifts, opened by the police. Haledjian studied a book on underwater treasure hunting from Abe Merkin; a pair of ski poles from Curt Gowan; a speargun from Jim Shick; and a monogrammed pith helmet from Walt Parker.

"Kirk's been living off his reputation for years," said the inspector. "He taught water skiing and skin diving to celebrities. Maybe if he'd stuck to his line he'd still be alive.

"He was a schemer. Never told anybody what he was up to, certainly not about the rendezvous with May Elliot. He invited four men to his birthday party here; they showed up, but he didn't, because that night he registered at the ski lodge under a phony name.

"I spoke with the four men," the inspector went on. "Kirk wrote them the same invitation: 'Before I go off skiing, come over and wish me a happy birthday. Tuesday. My place. 8:00 P.M.' The guests — Merken, Gowan, Shick, and Parker — left their gifts with the building superintendent and went home. They all claim they didn't know where he was going skiing."

"One of them is obviously lying," said Haledjian. *Which one?*

Curt Gowan, whose gift of ski poles showed he knew Kirk, the water-ski ace, was going to ski on snow when he should have assumed, as the others did, that he was going south to ski on water.

The Case of the
Murdered Wife

Dr. Haledjian finished examining the body of Maureen Page which lay on the maroon carpet of her fashionable Gables home.

"Mrs. Page was struck fatally on the head with the butt of that pistol," the famous sleuth said. "She probably was hit four or five times."

The .38 had been found near the body. Sheriff Monahan was carefully dusting it for fingerprints.

"I've telephoned her husband at his office," the sheriff said. "I only told him he'd better hurry home. Hate the job of breaking the news of her murder. Will you do it?"

"All right," Haledjian agreed heavily, watching the body being carried to an ambulance. Then he sat down to wait for John Page.

The ambulance had driven off when the distraught husband burst through the front door. "What happened? Where's Maureen?"

"I'm sorry to have to tell you this. She was murdered about two hours ago," said Haledjian. "Your cook found the body in the living room and telephoned the sheriff."

"I can't find fingerprints on the murder gun," interrupted the sheriff, holding the weapon wrapped in a handkerchief. "I'll have the lab go over it thoroughly."

Page's facial muscles twitched with emotion as he stared at the outline of the gun through the handkerchief. Suddenly he gripped the sheriff's arm. "Find the fiend who clubbed Maureen to death. I'll put up a fifty-thousand-dollar reward!"

"Save your money," said Haledjian. "The murderer won't be that hard to find!"

Why not?

Had John Page been innocent, he would not have known that his wife had been "clubbed" to death. Seeing the murder gun, he should have assumed she had been shot.

The Case of the
Murdering Rival

"Molly Fipps was murdered in the basement of her apartment house yesterday," Inspector Winters told Dr. Haledjian.

"The murder weapon, a bread knife, was wiped clean of fingerprints. But we have two suspects, Dereck Comin and Eric Hoder, a pair of rival suitors."

The inspector related the details of the case.

"Molly's body, dressed in sneakers, shorts, and a white sweatshirt, was found by the janitor at noon, about an hour after the time of death. She had been duly registered as a crew member aboard Derek Comin's yacht for the ocean powerboat race that afternoon. She'd been in his crew before.

"Comin got to the docks around noon, an hour late. He claims he was delayed by motor trouble, which he fixed himself. Nobody saw him do it. He could have spent the hour killing Molly.

"Eric Hoder was seen talking to Molly that morning in front of her apartment. He claims he asked her to lunch. He says she refused because she had an afternoon engagement and had to hurry to the hairdresser.

"Hoder, an artist, says he then went back to his studio and painted all day. But he has no confirming witnesses either.

"I talked to Comin and Hoder for hours," concluded the sheriff. "I can't shake their stories. One of them is lying, I'm sure of it."

"So am I," said Haledjian.

Whom did Haledjian suspect?

Haledjian knew Hoder lied in saying Molly told him earlier she was going to the hairdresser. No woman who was going yachting would have her hair set!

The Case of the
Musical Thief

The visiting British Army Band, under the baton of Sir Roger Lindsey-Haven, had just struck up "God Save the Queen" when two gunshots rang out.

Dr. Haledjian and Inspector Winters remained in their places until the anthem ended. Then they raced up the aisle and into the streets of New York City.

Two blocks away they found three policemen subduing a stocky man in a blue suit. One of the policemen reported to the inspector:

"The concert hall box office was held up a few minutes ago by a thickset masked man in a blue suit. He put six thousand dollars and his gun into a paper bag and fled.

"We spotted this fellow walking too quickly. When we ordered him to halt and he didn't, we shot into the air. He broke into a run and hurled a paper bag down the sewer."

"You're crazy!" screamed the prisoner. "I haven't

been past the concert hall! I heard a band playing 'God Save the Queen,' and somebody shouted, 'Halt or I'll shoot.'

"I haven't done anything," he insisted. "I figured the police were after somebody else. I heard shots so I ran to get off the street. I tossed a bag of orange peels into the sewer, not money! I got excited."

Just then the concert resumed. Despite the intervening buildings, strains of a march could be heard distinctly.

"You have a good ear for music," commented Haledjian. "And good eyes. There's a poster over the box office announcing tonight's performance of the British Army Band. You'd have done better not to have read it!"

What did Haledjian mean?

The prisoner insisted he had not been near the concert hall. Yet he never would have called the anthem he heard "God Save the Queen" unless he had seen the poster and knew a British band was performing.

Had he been innocent, he would have named the music by its American words, "My Country, 'Tis of Thee."

The Case of
Newton the Knife

As the headwaiter seated Dr. Haledjian and Octavia in a secluded corner, the sleuth observed a diner at the next table catch a squirt of grapefruit in his left ear.

"Puts me in mind of the case of Newton the Knife. Care to hear about it?" said Haledjian.

"Couldn't we order first?" asked Octavia.

"Newton the Knife," began Haledjian, hardly noticing the interruption, "was a notorious cutthroat. His body was found in a dingy Brooklyn bar. A bullet had entered his left ear and lodged midway in his brain, causing death instantly.

"The bullet matched the gun of Figaro Jones, another hoodlum and Newton's sworn enemy.

"Figaro said he was the last customer in the bar at closing time when Newton entered, raised his famous knife above his head, and, cursing in Russian, ran at him.

"Figaro claimed he shot in self-defense as Newton charged him head-on, like a maddened bull. Newton's knife was found clutched in his right hand. He apparently fell, holding it as he died.

"Figaro's self-defense plea was seconded by the bartender, the only eyewitness. But even without the bartender's phony corroboration, I knew Figaro's account was pure fabrication," concluded Haledjian. "Can you think why?"

"I'm too hungry to think," said Octavia. "Why? *Why?*"

It would have been impossible for Figaro to shoot Newton through the ear while Newton was charging him "head-on."

The Case of the
Office Shooting

As Inspector Winters looked around the cubby-hole office of John Stahl, Bart Rea said, "I touched nothing — except the desk telephone. I called you right away."

John Stahl's body lay on the threadbare carpet behind his desk. Near his right hand was a large French pistol.

"Tell me what happened," snapped the inspector.

"John asked me to come here," began Rea. "Then right off he started raving about his wife and me.

"I told him he was way out. But John has a red-flag temper. I couldn't calm him down. He doesn't know what he's doing when he goes crazy mad.

"Suddenly he jumped up and shouted, 'I'm going to kill you!' With practically one motion he yanked open the top drawer of his desk and took out a gun and fired at me. He missed. I shot back immediately. It was self-defense."

The inspector inserted a pencil into the barrel of the big French pistol and lifted it from beside the corpse. Opening the top desk drawer, he thoughtfully slid the gun inside.

"Rea's a private investigator," the inspector told Dr. Haledjian that night. "His pistol is registered to him. It fired the death bullet."

"We found a bullet from the French pistol in the wall opposite the desk — the shot Rea says Stahl fired first. The pistol bears Stahl's fingerprints, but he didn't have a license for it, and we can't trace it."

"You charged Rea with murder, I hope?" said Haledjian.

"What else could I do? He's already confessed."

What was Rea's slip?

Rea claimed that he had "touched nothing," and that Stahl "with practically one motion" had opened the drawer, taken out the gun, and fired.

Even a less hot-tempered man would never have bothered to close the drawer after pulling out a gun with intent to kill. The inspector found the drawer closed, remember?

The Case of the
Open Door

Working calmly and efficiently, Greg Verner hanged Brendon Trom in the attic of Trom's rented house. It was not until Verner tried to shut the front door that he hit a snag. The lock was jammed.

"Better get out of here," he thought, casting anxious glances at the dense woods surrounding the house.

Two hours later he was driving back to the house with Dr. Haledjian.

"Brendon's been morose since his divorce. I should have visited him, but nobody knew where he was hiding out. I got his address this afternoon when he telephoned me to say he was contemplating suicide. I thought you'd better come with me and perhaps have a talk with him.

"He said it was a white stucco house, 621 Delaware Avenue, over the phone," went on Verner. "Here we are."

111

Haledjian left the car first. Finding the front door ajar, he entered and switched on the lights. Five minutes later the two men found Brendon Trom in the attic.

As they stood silently staring at the body, a door chime sounded downstairs.

With Haledjian right behind him, Verner hastened to the back door. There stood a teenage girl. "Mother asked me to return this bottle of milk to Mr. Trom," she said.

Haledjian took the milk and after she had gone he called the police.

"You'd better arrest Mr. Verner on suspicion of murder," he said when they arrived.

Why?

Although Verner carefully built up the impression he had never visited the Trom house before, he knew while standing in the attic that the chime was from the back door.

The Case of the
Orange Bird

For years Mrs. Sydney, the wealthiest dowager in New York City, had vainly tried to outwit Dr. Haledjian. As the famous criminologist selected a cigar from the tray held by the Sydney butler, a wicked gleam came into his hostess's eye. It was time for playing stump-the-detective. . . .

"John DeMott, Paul Houk, and Lee Roach were partners in a successful New York jewelry business," began Mrs. Sydney. "Last January they flew down to the Florida Keys to spend a month at DeMott's lodge.

"One afternoon DeMott took Houk, an avid fisherman but a nonswimmer, out on his forty-foot cruiser. Roach, whose hobby was bird-watching, remained behind.

"Roach says he was sitting behind the lodge when he spied an exotic orange bird, belonging to a species new to him, fly by. He followed it to the front of the

113

house, and through binoculars watched it building a nest, high in a palm tree.

"Quite by chance, he moved the binoculars out to the water and saw DeMott and Houk struggling on the yacht. Roach says DeMott shoved Houk overboard and held his head under water.

"DeMott claimed that Houk had leaned over the side to gaff a fish, and, losing his balance, fell into the ocean. He drowned before DeMott could reach him.

"The coroner ascribed death to drowning. At the trial, it was simply DeMott's word against Roach's.

"The jury deliberated less than five minutes," concluded Mrs. Sydney. "No doubt, my dear doctor, you won't need so long to realize who was lying."

Haledjian didn't. Do you?

Although an experienced bird-watcher, Roach didn't know his tropical flora. Obviously, he didn't watch a bird building his nest in a palm tree as he claimed. Palm trees don't have branches, only long slippery fronds; and birds can't perch — much less nest — on them.

The Case of the
Overheard Killer

Steve Corrigan, the mad-dog killer, was shot to death in a Detroit boarding house during a gun battle with police, who acted on an anonymous telephone tip.

Two days earlier a man had held up a Toledo bank and slain two cashiers. A guard spotted a scar on the masked gunman's right hand. Within an hour the police had the telltale description booming over the loudspeakers of every transportation center within a fifty-mile radius of the crime.

Everyone with an eye to collecting the well-publicized fifty-thousand-dollar reward began insisting he was the anonymous tipster. The Detroit police asked Dr. Haledjian to screen the claimants.

The first was Bill Kempton, who told his story confidently.

"Just as my brother Carl boarded the bus to Bowling Green, the description came over the bus depot's

115

loudspeaker. Carl got a seat in the back, and as the bus started, he noticed a man with a scar on his right hand sitting midway up the bus.

"The man leaned over and said to the red-headed woman across the aisle, 'I'd better get off at the first stop and head for Detroit.'

"Carl's a deaf-mute and can read lips. He saw the scarred man pass the woman a note and say, 'Meet me in two days at this address.'

"Carl had me telephone the police anonymously when he got home. He had seen the red-haired woman crumple the note after reading it and drop it on the floor. Carl was the last off the bus and he picked it up. Here it is."

"It's the address of the boarding house where the killer was shot by the police, all right," said Haledjian. "Just as the newspapers gave it. Bring the next tipster, sergeant!"

What was wrong with Kempton's story?

The note was an obvious fake. Carl, the "deaf-mute," might be able to read lips and so know what the scarred man said. But Carl never could have attached importance to his remarks unless he had heard Corrigan's description broadcast over the depot loudspeakers as he boarded the bus.

The Case of the
Parked Car

The sleek foreign convertible was like many others in the Midcity garage except for the dead man's brown shoes and socks protruding from the opened driver's door.

"He was J. William Clancy, New York's top expert on men's fashions," Inspector Winters told Dr. Haledjian. "I sent for you because something is odd about this case.

"Here's what we've got," continued the inspector. "Clancy had a date for 8 P.M. with Denise Mills, a model, two nights ago. When he didn't show up, she telephoned his roommate, Kurt Wagner. Wagner checked on Clancy's movements.

"Wagner turned up nothing and called us. After backchecking, we found Clancy's body. It looks like Clancy was about to take out his car for the date with Miss Mills when another car hit him and kept going. Clancy dragged himself to the telephone in his car, but died before he could use it."

Haledjian bent over the body. He carefully studied the blood which had flowed from a corner of the dead man's mouth and dried upon his striped shirt and brown suitcoat lapel.

"Notice his watch," said the inspector. "It's smashed — the hands stopped at 7:45. The medical examiner says he died about forty-eight hours ago. That ties in — forty-eight hours ago Clancy was headed for his 8 P.M. date with Miss Mills."

"Quite wrong, inspector," said Haledjian. "The smashed watch is an inept attempt to misrepresent the time of death. Unquestionably Clancy died at least two hours earlier."

Haledjian straightened and stepped from the body. "The clumsy cover-up indicates Clancy was murdered!"

How did Haledjian know?

Only a man ignorant of fashion would have worn brown shoes, brown suit, and a striped shirt for a date at 8 P.M. After dark, Clancy, the fashion expert, would have worn black shoes, white shirt, and a dark suit.

The Case of the
Payroll Truck

Driving through deserted farm country a few miles from Fort Olmstead, Dr. Haledjian suddenly came upon an army truck that had crashed into a tree beside the road.

As he stopped his car, a jeep came from the opposite direction carrying two officers and two sergeants, all wearing side arms. A sergeant leaped out of the jeep and ran to the truck.

"They've been shot, major!" he shouted.

"I'm a doctor," said Haledjian. He opened the cab door. The driver was dead; the soldier beside him was dying.

"I can't do anything for them," murmured Haledjian to the major who had hurried over. The famous sleuth saw the cross on the officer's collar. "This is your work now, chaplain."

The major nodded and moved to the dying man.

The other officer, a captain, said to Haledjian,

"That's the fort's payroll truck. The way I see it, those poor boys were ambushed, but the driver managed to keep going till he died.

"Sergeant," the captain said. "Get the money out of the truck and put it in the jeep."

When the money had been transferred, the captain said, "Chaplain, you'd better stay here. We'll get help back to you as fast as we can. And don't trust anybody, you hear?"

The captain and the two sergeants sped off in the jeep. Haledjian waited only until they were around a bend to flatten the chaplain with a straight right to the jaw.

Why?

Haledjian realized the chaplain would shoot him and take off in his car the moment he saw his chance. The four soldiers were obviously impostors, as all were "wearing sidearms," including the chaplain. But service chaplains are forbidden to carry weapons.

The Case of the
Phantom Killer

"This one gives me the shudders," admitted Sheriff Monahan. "The killer operated on a split-second timetable, yet he apparently picked his victim at random.

"Brentwood Hills is just a two-minute stop on the express run to Kansas City," continued the sheriff. "The killer got off the train and walked into the two-room station. Tim Doherty was inside his office with Reverend Archibald. The office is separated from the outer room, or waiting room, by a swinging door set two feet off the ground. The two men were standing close to it, reading a church pamphlet.

"From where he stood in the waiting room, the killer could see only the trouser cuffs and shoes of the two men, and both were wearing blue trousers and black shoes. Yet he put all three bullets on the right side of the door, where Doherty was.

"The minister didn't hear a report, which means

that the killer either had a silencer or timed his shots with the screams of the locomotive whistle, or both. Doherty collapsed, and by the time Reverend Archibald had time to look, the train was pulling out. The killer had to be on it since there wasn't anybody in sight.

"We checked with the railroad people. Nobody bought a ticket to Brentwood Hills. Nobody, as far as we could determine, got off or on there.

"So it comes up this way," concluded the sheriff heavily. "A psycho picks a small town, slips off the train unnoticed, kills someone he never sees, and somehow slips aboard again. We'll never get him in a million years."

"Quite wrong, inspector," disagreed Haledjian. "After all, we don't have more than a dozen or so suspects to sift through."

What did Haledjian mean?

Haledjian knew that the killer in two minutes had to be able to: get on and off a train without attracting notice, know the duration of train whistles, and, most revealing of all, identify his victim merely by glancing at his shoes.

He was, therefore, a Pullman porter.

The Case of the
Phony Financier

"Last week I pulled off my best act yet," groaned Cyril Makin, the backfiring ladykiller. "I can't figure out how Ginger Faulk knew I was bluffing."

Makin flopped despondently into an armchair in Dr. Haledjian's study and recounted his latest tale of curdled courtship.

"Ginger's father is head of Affiliated Banks of California. She's accustomed to million-dollar deals being closed on the telephone.

"I decided to trump anything she'd ever heard on Mr. Bell's business line. So I had her meet me at noon for lunch in Behlen's, the swankiest restaurant in Los Angeles.

"After we had ordered, I called for a table phone. I asked to talk with Northern Airlines at Kennedy Airport, New York.

"John Gotch, an old buddy, was at the other end of the line, speaking from Behlen's kitchen. 'Page

Mr. Leonard Coffin,' I said. 'It's urgent!'

"After three minutes, John came on again as Coffin.

" 'We got the Western award,' I said. 'Tell Gristoffolis in Zurich the deal — reoffer the bonds at 99½ percent for the fifteen-year maturity. The selling commission of 1 percent on the long bonds and ½ percent on the short ought to net three million.' Then I hung up.

" 'Coffin,' I explained to Ginger, 'is taking the 1 P.M. flight to Zurich. By suppertime I should have the European cartel's answer.' "

"You were lucky," commented Haledjian, "Miss Faulk didn't throw something at you."

What was Makin's slip?

Because of the three-hour difference in time between the coasts, Makin's call, made in Los Angeles around noon, would have missed Coffin, flying at 1 P.M. from New York, by two hours.

124

The Case of the
Post Office Box

"Don't tell me Joey de Santos just handed over the Pondfield necklace to you!" bellowed Inspector Winters.

Nick the Nose backed against the wall of the inspector's office. "Now wait," he begged. "It wasn't like that. See this key? It's to Joey's mailbox in the Maple Street post office."

The greasy little informer shifted his feet nervously.

"You been looking for the Pondfield necklace, ain't you?" he asked. "Old man Pondfield insured it for a million. I bet the insurance company is breathing down your neck."

"The insurance people want the police to recover the necklace," admitted the inspector. "What are you selling?"

"The necklace," said Nick grandly. "Before the

cops shot him onto a slab, Joey mailed the necklace to his postal box — "

"Nuts!" exclaimed the inspector. "Are you telling me Joey just made you a present of his mailbox key?"

"No," said Nick quickly. "Last month when he was hiding after the Rockland job, he sent me out to a hardware store to have his car keys duplicated. Gave me his whole key ring. I duplicated everything on it, and kept the extras for myself. Just in case.

"When Joey got riddled yesterday, and the necklace ain't anywhere, I begin to think. Sure enough, one of the keys I had made fits his mailbox. The necklace is in one of them insulated bags. Now I figure it's worth — "

Nick the Nose's voice halted in a gasp as the inspector lifted him by the seat of the pants. Dr. Haledjian, who was coming into the office, held the door wide for one of Nick's headfirst departures.

Why did Nick the Nose get the heave-ho?

Nick the Nose struck out in stating he had the key to Joey's mailbox duplicated at a hardware store. No keysmith will duplicate a United States post office key.

The Case of the
Puzzled Hairdresser

"I can't figure out who learned I was taking the week's receipts to the bank on Thursday, a day early," said Mr. John, the hairdresser. "Every week for the past eight years I've taken the money at noon on Friday."

"Stop worrying," said Dr. Haledjian, as he finished bandaging Mr. John's head. "You're lucky to be alive. Whoever waylaid you in the alley must have used a piece of lead pipe."

"What I don't understand is who knew I was going, and where," said Mr. John.

"Whom did you tell?"

"Only my wife, Clara. At two o'clock I told her I was going to the bank."

"Did anyone overhear you?"

"There were three customers in the shop — new ones. I didn't even speak with them. Clara took care of two of them, and my brother Ted did the other.

I recall all three women were seated under hair driers, watching me, when I spoke with Clara about going to the bank."

"Where was Ted?"

"Out on a coffee break," replied Mr. John. "It couldn't have been either Ted or Clara."

"If you're so positive," said Haledjian thoughtfully, "we have only one suspect."

"Who?"

"Why, the one who couldn't possibly have overheard you if you screamed at the top of your lungs," replied Haledjian.

Whom did Haledjian mean?

None of the three women sitting under the hair driers could have heard Mr. John tell his wife he was going to the bank; hair driers simply make too much noise.

Therefore, Haledjian knew it had to be the woman who was deaf — and who could read lips.

The Case of the
Racketeer's Death

"The life policy on Mugsy McGurk, the labor racketeer, has a no-murder clause," said Henderson, the insurance investigator.

"You mean that if it turns out someone killed him, your company won't have to pay a cent?" asked Dr. Haledjian.

"Correct," acknowledged Henderson. "That's why I need your help. I can only suspect murder. Here are the few facts I have.

"McGurk died on the train to Miami. He had imbibed heavily in the club car until midnight. Then, helped by a waiter, he staggered to his berth, a lower in car 1056, and lay down without undressing. In a drunken stupor, he accidentally asphyxiated himself by burying his head in the pillow — or so it would seem.

"When he was found in the morning," continued Henderson, "his mouth and nose were clear of the pillow. It is thought he rolled when the train made a jolting halt about 1 A.M.

"A conductor had stopped the train — pulled the emergency cord — because he saw a man jumping off the last car. The man could have been McGurk's killer. Come into the next room, doctor. You'll see everything taken from McGurk's berth."

Haledjian viewed the articles piled on a square table. Besides the sheets, blankets, and a pillow belonging to the Pullman company, there was a mound of McGurk's clothes. Also the contents of his overnight bag. Among the latter were a pair of white pajamas, bedroom slippers, and a yellow bathrobe.

"Not much," conceded Henderson, "to prove murder."

"One article proves it," corrected Haledjian. *What was the article?*

Haledjian reasoned the killer had smothered McGurk with a pillow and then, fearing it held his fingerprints, took it with him. The article that gave the killing away was the pillow — the missing one. All train berths are made up with two.

130

The Case of the
Reluctant Witness

Dr. Haledjian and Sheriff Monahan walked slowly down the path that stretched between James Ernst's newly painted rear porch and his toolshed in the backyard.

"From any place along this path," said Sheriff Monahan, "Ernst could have seen Fred Kolp being slain. He's our only possible witness, but he denies seeing anything."

"What do you make of these?" asked Haledjian, pointing to the drops of white paint that had fallen in a line along the path.

"Ernst," answered the sheriff, "had finished painting his porch and was bringing the paint can to the shed about the time the killing took place. Ernst claims he didn't realize the can had sprung a leak till he got into the toolshed."

Haledjian examined the paint drops more carefully.

From the porch to about midpoint along the path the paint had fallen in nearly circular drops every three feet. From midpoint to the tool shed, the drops were spaced about nine feet apart and were longer and narrower.

Haledjian was not surprised to find the padlock hanging from the inside latch of the toolshed.

"Ernst is absolutely terrified," said the sheriff. "He's clammed up tight. If he knows more than he's telling, I'll have to prove he saw Fred Kolp slain to make him talk."

"No doubt he fears the killer's vengeance if he admits having seen the murder," said Haledjian. "But he saw it, all right!"

How did Haledjian know?

The drops of paint told Haledjian that Ernst was midway along the path when he saw the killing. From that point to the tool shed — where the latch on the inside indicated he had locked himself in — the drops were spaced farther apart and were longer and narrower, showing he had suddenly broken into a run.

The Case of the
Rescue at Sea

"Thank heaven you saw me!" exclaimed Tom Bond as he feebly helped make fast his battered yawl to Dr. Haledjian's chartered fishing boat.

Haledjian reached over the side and assisted the bedraggled yachtsman aboard.

Bond staggered into the shade of the cabin and sagged upon a berth. He removed his cap to wipe the perspiration from his brow, revealing a bald, freckled head.

"Drink this," said Haledjian, holding out a cup of water.

Bond gulped it frantically, asked for a second, and when he had downed it, told of his ordeal.

"Ben Page and I were sailing for Bimini when the storm hit us. The sails, rudder, and radio went in the first five minutes. We barely managed to keep afloat.

"We drifted five days, lost. Three days ago our

fresh water supply gave out. Ben went crazy with the heat and thirst. He started to drink the ocean water. I tried to restrain him — I hit him. He — he struck his head against the starboard rail. He's dead! It's my fault!"

Haledjian climbed into Bond's disheveled yacht. In the little cabin he found Ben Page laid out on his back, dead. The criminologist studied the bruise on Page's jaw and the one at the base of his skull.

Back on the fishing boat, he warned Bond grimly, "You're going to have to tell the police a better tale than the one you told me!"

Why didn't Haledjian believe Bond?

Haledjian knew that Bond's story of hitting Page and accidentally killing him while restraining him from drinking ocean water was false. If the supply of fresh water had given out "three days ago," as Bond claimed, he would have been dehydrated, and therefore could not have wiped "the perspiration from his brow."

The Case of the
Sealed Room

On the evening of April 1, Dr. Haledjian was dining with Octavia when he saw a waiter slip on the glassy surface of the dance floor and land amid a welter of broken dishes, stuffed lobster, and very tossed salad.

"Puts me in mind of the famous sealed room case," said Haledjian. "Want to hear about it?"

"I'd rather dance," said Octavia. "But go ahead."

"H. Henderson Calborn III, the eccentric millionaire," began Haledjian, "had a windowless room in his mansion sealed off. In this impregnable repository he kept only one item — the greatest treasure of his entire fortune — the sarcophagus of Tutomkin IV, Pharaoh of Egypt.

"One night Calborn heard a noise within the room. It sounded like somebody was moving the sarcophagus! The next morning he had welders burn open the six-inch steel door.

"Lo, the sarcophagus was gone!

"Rushing into the room, Calborn slipped and fell flat on the floor. From this uncommon position he could closely observe another phenomenon. The entire floor had been freshly varnished!

"He called me immediately. Examining the room, I perceived the difficulty of anyone entering by the steel door and then vanishing with a four-ton sarcophagus. When I asked Calborn if he had any enemies, he named two — Klondike Kate and Indian Joe.

"Now," concluded Haledjian, "keeping in mind today is April Fools' Day, can you tell me how I deduced which was the thief?"

"Being a fool doesn't help me," sighed Octavia. "Which one?"

Can you guess?

Indian Joe, the "varnishing American." (Ugh!)

The Case of the
Shattered Door

The 6-foot-4, 240-pound body of Earl Moon lay on the tile veranda amid a welter of shattered glass.

Dr. Haledjian studied the left side of Moon's jaw, which was bruised outside and bloody inside from a cut caused by two broken teeth. The bruise on the back of the head showed where Moon had struck the tiles. The back of the dead man's sports jacket was stitched with glass splinters.

"Apparently somebody punched Moon awfully hard on the side of the jaw," mused Haledjian. "Moon was thrown backward and he crashed through the closed sliding glass door. Falling, he struck his head on the veranda tiles and died of a broken neck."

"That confirms the account we have from Buster Epps, a neighbor," said Inspector Winters.

Epps moved from behind the inspector and stared

in disbelief at the body. He still seemed in a state of shock.

"I was tending my roses about half an hour ago when I noticed Moon and a stranger standing near this glass door. The stranger was not quite so tall as Moon, but just as broad. And he handled himself like a professional boxer.

"They seemed to be quarreling, but the door was shut and I couldn't overhear distinctly," continued Epps. "Suddenly Moon swung his fist. The stranger sidestepped expertly and hooked a left to Moon's jaw. Moon went crashing through the glass. He struck his head — I could hear the crack! The stranger fled immediately. I called the police when I couldn't overtake him."

"Now, now, Mr. Epps," said Haledjian. "Suppose you tell us what really happened."

Why didn't Haledjian believe Epps?

The stranger could not possibly have hit Moon on the left side of the jaw with a left hook. Had Moon exposed his left side, the natural blow would have been a right cross or a straight right.

The Case of the
Stamp Collector

"I came in to help Mr. Dunning to bed," said Brock, the aged family servant. "I found him like this and summoned you from the living room immediately."

The 85-year-old John Dunning, a noted philatelist, lay slumped over his desk, dead of a blow which had been struck to the base of the skull within the past five minutes.

"When I entered, I thought I heard the rear door close," said Brock. "It leads to a back stairway."

Haledjian examined the five objects on the desk. There were a pair of tweezers, a stamp album, a stamp catalogue, and a bottle of benzine with an eyedropper for use in detecting watermarks. A quartz floor lamp cast eerie ultraviolet rays over the dead man's left shoulder.

"Mr. Dunning had been appraising a stamp collection for a friend this evening," Brock explained.

Haledjian walked out of the room onto the balcony overlooking the living room, where the costume party, given by Dunning's granddaughter, was in sway.

"Who benefits from his will?"

"Why, I do," replied Brock. "And everyone at the party."

Haledjian studied the costumed merrymakers till his eye fell upon a young man dressed as Sherlock Holmes. His deerstalker's cap tipped rakishly, he was examining the eyes of a pretty Salome through a large magnifying glass while blowing smoke from a meerschaum pipe.

"Call the police," Haledjian told Brock, "while I detain Mr. Holmes for questioning."

How come?

Haledjian realized the murder weapon was the one object missing from the stamp expert's desk — a magnifying glass.

The Case of the
Sticky Brush

"Thanks for the lift into town, Dr. Haledjian," said Joe May. "Mind stopping at Al Pohl's?"

"Not a bit," replied Haledjian, turning into a side road that led to Pohl's house of red brick with white wood porch, steps, and windows.

"I've been meaning to contact Al for two days," said May. "I need the wrench he borrowed last week."

Haledjian had barely brought the car to halt when May hopped out. "Won't be a second," he called, racing across the lawn and leaping over the steps. He skidded on the slate floor of the porch, but righted himself quickly.

Getting no answer to the doorbell, he walked to a window and rapped on a pane. "Al?" he shouted. "Al?"

Suddenly, jumping off the porch, he screamed, "Dr. Haledjian! Be — behind the shrubs!"

To the left of the porch behind a long row of hibiscus set four feet from the brick wall, lay the body of Al Pohl. A six-foot stepladder had overturned on him. A can of white paint had spilled over his work shoes.

"Neck broken," said Haledjian. "About six hours ago."

The famous sleuth fingered the bristles of the paint brush near Al's right hand. "Sticky," he muttered.

Walking to the porch, he touched the white wood supports, the front door, the four steps, and the window sills. "Tacky," he said. "Al must have just finished painting them this morning when he met death."

The next day, after Joe May had been arrested, Haledjian told Sheriff Monahan:

"May thought that by pretending to discover the body with me he cleared himself of suspicion!"

What was May's error?

By saying, "I've been meaning to contact Al for two days," May expected to establish the fact that he hadn't been near the Pohl house during the killing. Yet the fact that he twice jumped over the steps and knocked on the window pane rather than the door revealed that he knew the steps and door had been newly painted.

The Case of the
Stolen Rubens

Unable to sleep, Dr. Haledjian was walking about the grounds of his host, Percy Kilbrew, former right-handed pitching great, when he noticed a limousine by the back door.

Suddenly a man, fully clothed, stepped out the door and passed the driver what appeared to be a painting. Then the man dashed into the house and the car roared off, bowling over a garbage can with enough noise to awaken the dead.

In the 4 A.M. darkness Haledjian could not identify the men or the car. But the fate of the Rubens oil was plain enough — it was missing from the living-room wall.

Haledjian sprinted upstairs to his host's room and received a prompt, "Come in," to his knock. Kilbrew stood half-clothed by a rumpled bed, his right leg in his trousers and his left leg out.

"I heard the clatter and was just getting dressed

143

to investigate," he said. "What happened?"

"The Rubens has been stolen," said Haledjian.

Kilbrew finished pulling on his trousers and followed Haledjian downstairs barefooted.

In a few minutes Kilbrew's three other house guests descended the stairs.

John Ward, the art critic, wore an Oriental robe over black silk pajamas. Marty Latham, the singer, wore an old-fashioned nightshirt and cap. Everette Maloski, the painter, wore only tattered pajama bottoms.

"The Rubens is heavily insured," said Kilbrew. "But I don't care about the money. I want the painting back!"

"You don't have a worry on that score," Haledjian assured him.

Whom did Haledjian suspect?

Kilbrew — of wanting the insurance money and the painting. Although he claimed to be "just getting dressed," he was really getting undressed, since his left leg was out of his trousers. A right-handed man usually takes his right leg out first when undressing; he invariably puts his left leg in first when dressing.

The Case of the
Suicide Room

Sir Cecil Brookfield pulled back a massive door that opened off one of the arched corridors in his six-hundred-year-old castle in Wales.

Dr. Haledjian, a weekend guest, peered down into darkness.

"A room with four walls — and no floor," said Sir Cecil. "Or rather, a floor one hundred feet below the threshold.

"The room was designed to dispose in secret of troublesome vassals," explained Sir Cecil. "Later, when the beautiful wife of the first Lord Brookfield died in the plague, a grief-stricken young forester hurled himself to his doom here.

"A nasty legend developed from the forester's death," added Sir Cecil slowly. "It is that a young man will jump in the reign of every fourth baron. I am the fourth since the last suicide."

Sir Cecil shoved the heavy door shut. "I've ordered a mason from the village. He'll be here tomorrow to seal off the door."

Haledjian's bedroom was three doors from the "suicide room." As he was retiring for the night, he heard an eerie, dull thud. It could mean only one thing. He hastened to the corridor.

Sir Cecil was running toward the "suicide room." Together the two men swung open the massive door. Sir Cecil played a flashlight down into the dark pit.

The beam revealed the body of a young man.

"Ritchie, my wife's solicitor!" gasped Sir Cecil. "Why should he take his own life?"

"He didn't," corrected Haledjian. "He was pushed!"

How did Haledjian know?

The door to the "suicide room" was found closed. As the room had no floor, it would have been impossible for Ritchie to have closed the massive door from the inside and then turned and jumped.

The Case of the
Telltale Clock

Police found the body of Buffalo Fenn in his tenement room. He had been strangled by the electric cord of his alarm clock. Set for seven-thirty, the clock had stopped at seven.

Inspector Winters had Pete "The Hangman" Skones, Buffalo's inveterate foe, picked up for questioning.

The Hangman claimed that on the morning of Buffalo's murder, he had been in the middle of a three-day poker game with underworld friends. The friends swore he never left the hotel room.

A week passed without a new lead. Then Nick the Nose wheedled his way into the inspector's office.

The greasy little informer grinned. "I got something."

"It had better be good," warned the inspector. "The last five times you got the boot."

"I got a witness to Buffalo's murder," announced Nick smugly. "Broadway Ben.

"Ben," said Nick, "had a room down the hall from Buffalo. He was passing Buffalo's room when he sees Buffalo's door ajar. He hears nothing at first but the ticking of Buffalo's alarm clock. And suddenly he don't hear even that.

"Then Ben hears a sound he don't like to hear at seven in the morning or any time else. He hides in a doorway at the end of the hall. Two minutes later he sees the Hangman scurry out of Buffalo's room and race downstairs.

"Ben is so scared after he reads what happened to Buffalo that he ain't looked at an alarm clock for a week. He's hiding, but I can take you to him for five grand. He'll testify."

"I don't pay for perjury," growled the inspector.

"He never improves," sighed Haledjian, entering the inspector's office and holding the door wide for Nick's flying exit.

Why was Nick booted?

Nick made too much of the ticking of the alarm clock, whose electric cord had been used to strangle Buffalo Fenn.
Alas for Nick, electric clocks don't tick.

The Case of the
Unused Seat Belt

When Inspector Winters slammed on the brakes, Dr. Haledjian would have been pitched through the windshield but for his seat belt.

The reason for the inspector's sudden stop was horribly evident.

A red sports car had come racing around the hairpin turn on the mountain road ahead. Out of control, the car had crashed through the guardrail.

The impact didn't stop the car, but it flung the driver straight up. He seemed to hang in the air a moment before plunging out of sight.

Haledjian and the inspector scrambled down the two hundred-foot precipice.

The driver's body was a shattered mass of broken bones and blood. About one hundred feet beyond, the sports car lay on its side, a total wreck.

"Strange," muttered the inspector, pointing to the seat belt, obviously unused, which lay in the fresh

149

blood that covered the driver's bucket seat.

"I doubt that even a seat belt could have saved his life," said Haledjian.

"I'd better telephone the state police," said the inspector. "It looks like one more traffic fatality for the year. Do you think he fell asleep at the wheel?"

"No," said Haledjian. "He was murdered."

Why murder?

The fact that blood soaked the driver's seat though he had been cast free of the car when it hit the rail indicated he had bled before the accident: i.e., he had been killed and placed in the car, which had then been sent down the mountain road.

The Case of the
Warehouse Murder

"I heard a man scream twice," said Bob Lovell, an unemployed dog trainer. "Naturally, I stopped and looked through the ground floor window of the Universal Tire Company warehouse. I saw Mike Denton dragging a man toward a stack of whitewall tires, maybe ten or twelve feet high. I telephoned the cops right away."

"You didn't go inside the warehouse?" asked Inspector Winters.

"No. Why, I wasn't ever near the building before," retorted Bob. "I was just out for a stroll. So what happens to a public-spirited citizen? He gets thrown in jail. Denton is your man, not me!"

The inspector nodded patiently. To the officer at the door he said, "Take Lovell back and bring in Mike Denton."

Denton, a laundry worker, admitted being inside the warehouse.

"I got an anonymous telephone call asking me to come there," he said. "The door was open, so I went in. I don't know nothing about a murder."

"Mel Capone's body, stabbed eight times, was found inside a twelve-foot-high stack of whitewall tires in the warehouse," said the inspector.

"The reason we found the body," continued the inspector, "was that the killer grew sloppy. He stacked the tires above Capone in a leaning column. The warehouse manager says he has his men pile the tires in perfect columns."

"I didn't kill Capone," blurted Denton. "I'm being framed!"

That night the inspector related the case to Dr. Haledjian.

"The warehouse workers," said the famous sleuth, "have picked out the killer for you, Inspector!"

What did Haledjian mean?

Lovell said he'd never been near the warehouse before. Yet he knew the tires toward which Capone was being dragged were whitewalls. From the window, he couldn't have seen anything but the treads, since the tires were stacked "ten or twelve feet high" by the warehouse workers in "perfect columns."

The Case of the
Whispering Finger

A policeman patrolling Midland Park heard the two shots and, racing toward the sounds, found the body of Willard Wilson sprawled on a little-used path near the boat basin. Wilson was dead of two bullet wounds in the head.

Sonny Dobein, an ex-convict seen in the park at the time of the murder, was held overnight by police, but released for lack of evidence. The dead man's widow immediately offered a fifty-thousand-dollar reward for the arrest of the killer.

The reward brought Nick the Nose, nostrils fluttering to the scent of fifty thousand dollars, into the office of Inspector Winters, who was discussing the case with Dr. Haledjian.

"I got a witness says Sonny Dobein fingered Wilson," announced the greasy little informer.

"You always have a witness for a price," snapped

153

the inspector. "For fifty grand you ought to have a dozen!"

"This is on the level," insisted Nick. "Listen, my witness was in the park when Wilson was killed. He sees two men on a bench. One of them, Sonny Dobein, whispers to the other, 'Wilson always takes this path.' My witness thinks it's kinda odd Dobein should whisper somethin' like that, but he keeps walkin'. Then he reads about the murder in the papers."

"He must have heard the two shots," growled the inspector. "Why didn't he speak up right away?"

"My witness is deaf, but he reads lips good," replied Nick quickly. "He can testify to what Dobein told the other man, the gunman, I figure, and the jury will — "

Nick the Nose finished the sentence out in the hall, where the inspector threw him.

Why?

Nick's alleged witness was deaf and couldn't hear two shots, yet he remembered what Dobein said to the gunman because he "whispered."

The Case of
Willie the Wisp

Dr. Haledjian was vacationing in Europe when Count Schwinn, head of customs in France, requested help on a "perplexing problem of suspected smuggling."

Schwinn had scarcely entered Haledjian's hotel suite when he blurted, "Are you acquainted with Eugene W. McNally?"

"Better known as Willie the Wisp?" asked Haledjian. "He fenced diamonds in America for years and never got caught."

"That's the man," replied Schwinn. "He's got a new game. Six months ago he showed up at our customs post at Durien driving a new black convertible Fiorta, a foreign car that costs eleven thousand dollars. Naturally, we checked every inch of it. Nothing. But each of his three pieces of luggage had a false bottom."

Schwinn shook his head in exasperation. "In the

155

false bottoms were three jars — one filled with molasses, one with ground oyster shells, and one with bits of colored glass. We couldn't hold him for hiding such things, naturally. Now twice a month here comes a big, black expensive Fiorta into the country at Durien. Willie again! Hidden in his bags are the jars filled with the same curious contents: molasses, glass, and shells.

"The brazen crook just sits and smirks at my customs men. They're forced to admit him into the country!" concluded Schwinn.

"Molasses, shells, and colored glass," mused Haledjian.

"What do they add up to?" cried Schwinn. "What's he smuggling?"

Haledjian lit a pipe and drew upon it reflectively. At length he grinned. "Deuced clever fellow, Willie."

What was Willie smuggling?

Willie the Wisp, a man with a shady reputation, knew he couldn't pass customs regularly without soon arousing suspicion, and he therefore created some. The jars and their contents, which baffled deduction, made sense to Haledjian as decoys. Hence Willie was smuggling black convertible Fiorta automobiles!

The Case of the
Wooden Bridge

Archie Tate, mayor of Hays, collapsed in the reviewing stand at the Veterans Day parade just as the army drill team marched past.

"Tate died within the hour of a bullet wound inflicted by a high-powered rifle," Sheriff Monahan told Dr. Haledjian the next day.

"Who hated Tate enough to kill him?" said Haledjian.

"Orv Prill, maybe — I took his statement." The sheriff lifted a sheet from his desk and read Prill's words:

"I was resting under the trees near the old wooden bridge when the army drill team passed over it. They were a sight to see, stepping in perfect unison, rifles shining, and buttons glistening in the overhead sun."

"Prill," said the sheriff, "claims he lay near the bridge and didn't walk the half mile into town till night. There wasn't anybody out there to verify his story. But nobody saw him in town, either."

"Why did the drill team cross the bridge on foot?"

"It's too rickety for those heavy army vehicles, so Lieutenant Cord had his men walk across," said the sheriff. "They joined the parade behind the high school band around noon."

"You think Prill knew beforehand the route the drill team was to take into town and made up an alibi about being there all afternoon?" asked Haledjian.

The sheriff nodded. "I believe he lied about seeing the soldiers cross the bridge. By then he had to be holed in town ready to shoot Tate.

"But," concluded the sheriff. "His story about the bridge is so simple it can't be disproved."

Haledjian disagreed. Do you?

No body of soldiers ever steps "in perfect unison" across a rickety old wooden bridge (as Prill claimed) for fear of setting up vibrations that might collapse the structure. Lieutenant Cord would have ordered a route step at the bridge.

MORE
TWO-MINUTE
MYSTERIES

For Kurt Severin

The Case of the
Airport Killing

"At 8 A.M. on Monday, March 4, 1968, you were drinking coffee in a rear booth in the Sandwich Shop at the airport?" asked the district attorney.

"I was," answered McCarthy, the murder defendant.

"And you didn't see the man in the booth across the aisle — not five feet from you — stabbed to death!"

"No, I was reading the local morning newspaper."

"The cashier remembers you. You were in an awful hurry. You gave her a half-dollar in payment of a 15-cent check, and you didn't wait for your change."

"I had to catch a plane."

"You were aware of the time, but you didn't notice the man in the next booth was dead — with a knife sticking out of his chest?"

"I might have seen him, but I never looked directly at him."

"You didn't hear him order eggs and coffee?"

"I might have. I don't remember. I was busy reading the New York Stock Exchange listings. I own some shares."

"How long did that take you?"

"A couple of minutes. Then I read the market news. There was a long article forecasting steel prospects for next year. After I finished reading the article, I noticed the time. I had less than two minutes to catch my plane to Los Angeles."

In the rear of the courtroom, Dr. Haledjian leaned over and whispered to Inspector Winters: "If he isn't convicted of murder, he'll draw a stiff sentence for perjury!"

How come?

The defendant claimed he was so busy checking stocks in the morning newspaper that he didn't notice the killing. Impossible!

On Monday, local morning newspapers do not carry stock exchange transactions.

The Case of the
Anxious Nephew

"I'm worried about my Uncle Phil." Stephen Bates' voice was anxious over the telephone. "He failed to keep a dinner engagement with me tonight. Do you mind meeting me at his place — say in half an hour?"

Dr. Haledjian agreed and he was waiting in the lobby of Philip Bates' apartment building when Stephen arrived by cab.

"My uncle thought he was being followed the last couple of days," said Stephen. "He keeps a great deal of cash in a wall safe in his den. Unfortunately, he isn't exactly secretive about it."

"Did you try to reach him tonight?" asked Haledjian.

"When he didn't show up for dinner, I telephoned his home. I got no answer."

Leaving the elevator on the fourteenth floor, the two men walked rapidly to the door of Philip Bates' bachelor apartment. It was unlocked. In the entrance hall burned the only light.

"Better have a look in the den," suggested Haledjian.

Stephen nodded and led the way. He paused at the door to the darkened room. "There's a floor lamp in the corner," he said, and disappeared into the darkness. An instant later the room was bathed in light. Directly behind the desk a small oval safe door was open. Stephen stood in a corner, one hand on the lamp, an expression of alarm twisting his face. He stepped back over the unmoving form of his uncle, who lay at his feet. "I-is he dead?"

Haledjian knelt beside Philip Bates. "No, a nasty blow on the head, but not fatal — lucky for you! You went to a lot of trouble to throw me off the scent. Then at the last minute you practically confessed to the crime!"

What was Stephen's mistake?

In leaving the floor lamp, Stephen had "stepped back over" his uncle. Thus, in going to the lamp, he'd had to step over his uncle, which he did. But only a man who knew beforehand that Philip Bates lay on the floor could have avoided tripping over him in the darkness.

168

The Case of the
Arctic Hero

"Don't tell me," said Dr. Haledjian. "Let me guess. You made a play for a young lady, but got your lines fouled and your face slapped."

Cyril Makin, the luckless Lothario, nodded glumly. "This time I was absolutely sure I had my story down pat. Yet something went wrong. I can't figure what.

"You've heard of Gertrude Morgan?" he asked. "Her grandfather sailed with Admiral Byrd and a cousin climbed Mt. Everest with the Eggler party. If you haven't combed icicles from your whiskers, you don't rate with her.

"I took her to dinner Christmas Eve, and it seemed a good time to trundle out my Arctic Circle yarn," continued the youth. "I opened by commenting that I had once spent Christmas Eve in less comfortable surroundings.

"Then I told her about the morning Lt. Craven

169

and I were mushing back to the Navy's Arctic Observation Weather Station. Suddenly Craven fell and fractured his leg. Ten minutes later the stretch of ice we were crossing broke loose. We began to drift out to sea.

"I realized Craven and I and the dogs would freeze to death unless I started a fire. Alas, we had used up all of our matches. I got out a small magnifying glass from our instrument kit and, tearing off sheets from our reports, laid them on a steel instrument box. By focusing the sun's rays through the glass onto the paper, I started a hearty blaze.

"Fortunately, a cutter picked us up after 24 hours. The captain said I was a bit of a hero."

"But not Miss Morgan," said Haledjian. "And no wonder!"

What was wrong with Cyril's story?

In the Arctic Circle on Christmas Eve, Cyril could not have started a fire by using the sun's rays. As every student knows (or should), the sun disappears in the far north from October to about March.

The Case of the
Book Contract

"I should like a moment to scan the contract," said the scholarly, white-haired man who called himself Everett Willy. "If there is a major point of disagreement, I should prefer to know it now."

"Of course," agreed Morgan, the publisher. As Dr. Haledjian watched from the leather office couch, the publisher passed a contract of three sheets across his desk to Willy.

Haledjian observed Willy's eyes skim the lines of small type. The pages of the contract were flipped rapidly.

"It appears to be satisfactory," said Willy, putting the contract into his attaché case. "I shall have to read it carefully when I am home, you understand. Tomorrow you will have my answer."

Smiling, Willy rose, shook hands, and departed.

"All right," Haledjian said to Morgan. "Why did you ask me to sit in on a book contract discussion?"

"Twenty years ago," replied Morgan, "Everett Willy wrote a masterpiece on the English language; it's become the standard text on the subject. No one ever saw him, however. He was a man of mystery.

"For the past ten years there have been rumors that he was in South America working on a new book, better than the first. A month ago came rumors that the new book was done, but that Willy had died a few days after completing it. The man who presented himself to me just now has the manuscript — and it's superb! But is the man really Everett Willy? Or is he an imposter trying to profit from another man's manuscript?"

"An imposter!" answered Haledjian without hesitation.

What made Haledjian so sure?

The real Everett Willy, a master of the English language, would not have committed one of the most common errors in the language — misusing the word "scan."

The verb "to scan" means to examine intensively. The imposter, like most semieducated persons, thought it means "to skim" in reading.

The Case of the
Bottle of Cyanide

Arthur Maxim sagged in an easy chair. His right hand lay on his lap, clutched about a bottle of cyanide.

"He's been dead about fifteen minutes," Dr. Haledjian told Carter. "Have you called the police?"

"Yes — but I called you first. I knew you were at the hotel. Arthur was depressed, but — good heavens! — I never dreamed he'd kill himself!"

"You knew him well?" asked Haledjian.

"We were kids together," replied Carter. "Since his wife divorced him, he's been despondent. I suggested this vacation. He seemed better yesterday. We played golf and fished.

"Half an hour ago I went down to the lobby for a newspaper. Just as I returned, he drank that bottle in his hand."

Inspector Winters arrived. Haledjian summed up his findings.

"You'll notice how lax the body is," said the sleuth, pointing to the drooping position the corpse had assumed in the chair. "Cyanide kills instantly, and the muscles go limp.

"Maxim appears to have committed suicide by drinking cyanide. But no conclusion is possible till we know for certain the cause of death."

Two days later the inspector told Haledjian: "The lab confirms that Maxim's death was due to cyanide."

"That clinches it!" was the reply. "Arrest Carter on suspicion of murder!"

Why?

As cyanide "kills instantly, and the muscles go limp," Maxim couldn't possibly have held the bottle clutched in his hand. It had to have been put there after death!

174

The Case of the
Bullet in the Back

Dr. Haledjian and the tour's other saddle-sore dudes gazed down upon two rotting pieces of timber.

"Now this here spot," intoned their unshaven little guide, "is called Bushwack Alley, bein' so known for the shootin' of two deputies back in '73.

"Elbow Bend was a thrivin' town in them days, and Doc Pressman's house stood right here. One night there's some gunplay in back, and a stranger staggers into Doc's kitchen.

"The doc removes a .44 slug from the stranger's upper back, loans him a clean shirt, and fixes his right arm in a sling.

"Says the stranger: 'I was crossin' South Street when I heerd gun-fightin' and seen a fella runnin' from two lawmen. I joined the chase. The fella ambushed us in the deadend behind your house, Doc, killed the lawmen, and wounded me.'

"Just then Sheriff Pell and Clyde Everest, the local undertaker, storm in.

" 'I bet that's him!' cries Everest.

"The sheriff draws his gun. 'A gunslinger robbed the freight office and killed two of my best deputies, mister. Don't give me no trouble.'

" 'Hold on!' shouts the stranger. 'I was helpin' your deputies chase the real thief!'

" 'The bullet in your back says you was doin' the runnin', not the chasin',' " points out Everest.

"Seein' as there was no witnesses," concluded the guide, "the sheriff just naturally had to string up the stranger."

"Naturally," sighed Haledjian. "Whoever heard of a western sheriff hanging the guilty man!"

What was the basis for Haledjian's remark?

As there were no witnesses, Everest could not know the stranger had been shot in the back, unless Everest himself did the shooting. The stranger was wearing the doc's clean shirt when Everest, the real thief, saw him in the house.

The Case of the
Confederate Half-Dollar

Driving through a dilapidated neighborhood at midnight, Dr. Haledjian abruptly stomped on his brakes. His headlights had illuminated a man lying on the sidewalk.

The man still breathed, though strangulation marks on his neck indicated the sleuth's sudden arrival had scared off the assailant in the nick of time.

The street was deserted till an elderly man stepped from the door of a decaying building nearby.

"Why, it's old Keyes! I knew this would happen. I warned him!"

"Warned him about what?" demanded Haledjian.

"About going around jingling his Confederate half-dollar. I'm Stevens. Keyes and I have lived across the hall from each other for twenty years. Ten minutes ago I heard him go out — he jingles that half-dollar all the time, as if inviting somebody to rob him."

"Is the half-dollar valuable?"

"It is one of four made in 1861, and it's worth about $5,000," said Stevens. "Keyes kept it as a good luck charm. I've told him to be careful. Is it stolen?"

Haledjian refused to permit a search on the sidewalk. At the hospital, however, the coin was found in Keyes' right trouser pocket.

Haledjian telephoned Inspector Winters.

"The only other items Keyes carried were two handkerchiefs and a leather wallet containing a dollar bill," said the sleuth. "I suggest you arrest Stevens at once!"

How come?

Haledjian realized that Stevens, attempting to establish an alibi, claimed he had been in his room and that he knew Keyes had departed because he jingled his rare half-dollar.

Unfortunately for Stevens, Keyes carried nothing else in his pocket against which the rare coin could strike — and so jingle!

The Case of the
Department Store Murder

Dr. Haledjian was walking past the lingerie counters on the ground floor of a crowded department store when he was nearly gored by a bull.

"Sorry," apologized the slim young man in shirtsleeves. He bowed and proceeded on his way, agilely steering a papier-mâché bull's head through the mob of shoppers.

Behind him trailed two hefty girls ladened with the bull's hindquarters. They were followed by a procession of slender men: two brunets bearing matador costumes, a redhead carrying several black petticoats, and four blonds each lugging a bare manikin upside down.

Haledjian observed the parade of window dressers file into a roped-off area by the back of a display window. He thought nothing of them until an hour later, when he saw a crowd and several policemen collected by the window.

"Somebody murdered Joe Johnson, a store executive, as he sat at his desk," said Inspector Winters. "The only possible angle of fire leads back to this display window.

"The killer," added the inspector, "undoubtedly used a silencer. But what baffles me is why nobody saw him pull the gun."

"Perhaps I can help," said Haledjian, stepping outside to study the newly decorated window, which was designed to sell toreador pants at $39.98.

The four manikins, attired as matadors, stood around the papier-mâché bull. The background consisted of a screen painted to resemble a stadium filled with spectators.

"I believe I can recall the face of the murderer," Haledjian told the inspector. "Shall we go to your office and look through the albums?"

Whom did Haledjian suspect?

The redheaded man, who had apparently scooped up some petticoats from a counter and fallen in with the window dressers. As the petticoats had no place in the window, since toreador pants were shown, their only purpose was to conceal the gun!

The Case of the
Double Blowout

Dr. Haledjian was returning late at night from a hunting trip when the headlights of his car shone upon a sedan parked across the country road.

He swerved onto the shoulder to avoid a collision and braked as two of his tires blew. Suddenly four masked men appeared. They relieved him of his money and sped off in the sedan.

"A neat little caper," muttered the sleuth, playing his flashlight over the scattering of razor-sharp studs that had caused the two flats.

Tramping to a farmhouse, he told the farmer who answered his knocking, "I was just robbed about a mile down the road. I'll need a new tire. Can you get someone to help me?"

"Come in," the farmer invited. "I'll telephone Titusburg. Make yourself comfortable."

The farmer disappeared into the kitchen. Haledjian heard him speak over the telephone to the sheriff and then to a service station.

"The sheriff and a new tire are on the way here," the farmer said, emerging from the kitchen.

An hour later the sleuth was recounting the details of the holdup to the sheriff while a serviceman put on his spare tire and the new tire which the farmer had requested.

Then, upon Haledjian's recommendation, the sheriff arrested the farmer for being involved in the holdup.

Why?

Unless he had seen Haledjian's car, parked at night a mile from his house, the farmer could not have known what size tire to order.

The Case of the
Dying Brazilian

It had been months since Nick the Nose had slipped into Inspector Winters' office to peddle a phony tip.

"I got something on the Nilo Bernardes case," the greasy little informer confided slyly.

"Nilo Bernardes," the inspector explained to Haledjian, "is a 10-year-old boy who was kidnapped last month in Santos, Brazil. His father, a millionaire, paid the ransom. The boy has not been returned."

"Last night," said Nick, "this old guy in Pedro's Flop started to talk as he lay dying. At first he ran on about how he had lived all his life in Brazil and never did anything wrong till last month. Then he got interesting.

"He said he had sinned by collecting the ransom money for young Nilo. Before he got paid his share, he had overheard the rest of the kidnap gang plotting to kill him.

"So that night he stowed away on a freighter and jumped ship in America. With his dying breath, he named the town in Brazil where the kidnappers were laying low.

"Of course, he spoke in Spanish and I didn't understand him. But Pedro, who is Mexican, understood and did the interpreting. Pedro will back me up.

"I figure," concluded Nick, "that the name of the town where the kidnappers are hiding is worth a bundle!"

The inspector rose, growling. Haledjian barely had time to open the office door before Nick went sailing out.

Why was Nick given the heave-ho?

Nick the Nose had bribed Pedro, the flophouse proprietor, to confirm his phony tip.

However, a dying man who had "lived all his life in Brazil" wouldn't speak his last words in Spanish, but in Portuguese, the language of Brazil!

184

The Case of the
Escobi Sapphire

"The coroner just finished a preliminary examination," said Inspector Winters. "Professor Merton died of a heart attack about 11 P.M. I telephoned you because of a complication over the Escobi Sapphire."

"The ring given him by the Maharani of Isha during his trip to the East last year," recalled Haledjian.

"And worth an emperor's ransom," added the inspector. "Miss Samuels, Professor Merton's long-time secretary, claims he presented it to her last week. She kept it hidden in her room and told no one — afraid of causing family resentment. However, Anita Merton, a teenage niece, insists she saw her uncle wearing the sapphire an hour before he died."

"Thus the question is whether Miss Samuels received the sapphire as a gift, or by stripping it from

185

a dead man's hand," said Haledjian, as he examined the body.

Edwin Merton, lecturer in Rabbinic Hebrew, lay slumped in a heavy leather armchair. A red volume, open to reveal Hebrew print, lay where it had fallen at the moment of death.

Haledjian asked to see the niece, who told her story with cool assurance.

"I was in the den with Uncle between nine and ten o'clock," she said. "I had some typing to do, and he said I might go ahead, as he was merely reading for pleasure."

"From the red book by the chair?"

"Yes."

"And was he wearing the Escobi Sapphire?"

"He was. I sat here at the desk, not eight feet from him. I couldn't have been mistaken. Occasionally, when his right hand turned the page, the jewel, which he wore on his little finger, flashed brilliantly."

Haledjian's face tightened in a rare display of anger. "You are a jealous young lady. I suggest you go directly to Miss Samuels and apologize for maliciously attemping to discredit her."

Why?

The professor was reading a book written in Hebrew, which is read from "back to front." He therefore would not have turned the pages with his right hand, but with his left.

186

The Case of the
Fashion Cameraman

"I was taking fashion movies this morning when the men who held up the American Bank ran smack in front of the camera," Ed Courtney said over the telephone.

"Somebody broke into my studio this afternoon," he continued. "I'm sure it was the bank robbers. Luckily, the film was in the developer and they missed it. Can you come over? I may need help."

Dr. Haledjian assured the frightened man he was on his way. When he arrived, a movie projector was humming. The criminologist had a fleeting glimpse of a fashion model on the screen a split second before the film ran out with a snapping clack.

"I've got close-ups of the robbers near the start," said Courtney, flipping off the machine. Quickly he removed the reel and dropped it into a black bag.

"I'm off to the police with this," he said. "Would

you mind staying here, just in case those cutthroats are watching, while I sneak out the back?"

Haledjian agreed. "But be careful," he warned.

"Courtney wasn't careful enough," Sheriff Monohan told Haledjian three days later. "He drove off the road. His body was discovered in his wrecked convertible at the bottom of Gurnsey Ravine an hour ago, along with this."

The sheriff held up the reel of film. "Let's have a look at it," he said, threading a projector.

Courtney's pictures were professionally perfect — except they were entirely of skinny fashion models in bizarre clothes.

"There's the proof that Courtney was murdered," said Haledjian. "The bank robbers edited out the hold-up sequences and then tried to make his death look like an auto accident!"

What was Haledjian's proof?

Courtney had removed the film from his projector without rewinding it. Hence, unless it had been tampered with, the models would have been walking upside down and backwards when shown in the sheriff's office.

The Case of the
Fast Traveler

"Try the manual dial," suggested Dr. Haledjian, after Captain Gordon of the Miami police had punched all the push buttons of the radio and had got only static.

Immediately, music poured out noisily.

"Do you always play the radio so loud?" snapped Gordon at the pale youth riding handcuffed in the rear seat of the car.

"I play it any way I feel like. It's my convertible," retorted McGuire.

Haledjian turned down the volume. For the rest of the drive to headquarters he thoughtfully reviewed the case.

The Chicago National Bank had been held up four days ago, and more than half a million dollars was stolen. One of the holdup men, according to the Chicago Police Department's informer, was Billy McGuire, a young ex-convict. The informer said

McGuire had headed straight for Miami in a green convertible after the crime.

That morning the convertible had been spotted in the driveway of a big-time Florida gambler. The gambler swore the youth had been living with him in Miami for two months, and therefore couldn't have taken part in a Chicago robbery.

A search of the gambler's home disclosed McGuire's summer clothing in the guest room, and throughout the house a typical amount of underworld luxury, including a connoisseur's collection of popular records. But none of the stolen money.

"You're wastin' your time, Gordon," taunted McGuire. "Hey — tune up the radio. That's the Dixie Bobcats. Ain't they the greatest?"

"Like popular music, do you?" inquired Haledjian.

"I like a lot of things. Especially this Florida climate," sneered McGuire.

"Enjoy it while you can," answered Haledjian. "Once this car is back in Chicago, you and your gambler friend will have to think up a new alibi."

Why?

Two reasons: McGuire's lack of a suntan, and the fact that the push buttons of the car radio had not yet been adjusted to the Florida stations. They were still tuned to Chicago frequencies, as investigation later showed.

190

The Case of the
Fatal Slip

Dr. Haledjian parked his car and offered his services to the state trooper. The policeman was about to question one of the drivers involved in a tragic accident on the winding mountain road.

The driver was young, broad-shouldered, and dressed in evening attire that was spotless, except at the trouser cuffs and shoes. These were splattered with mud.

Dazedly he told his story.

"I was taking Joan to the dance. That other car crossed the centerline, forcing me wide. The road is slippery from the rain this morning, and I skidded off the embankment.

"Luckily," he continued, "I escaped injury when my car hit that tree. But Joan was knocked unconscious. I carried her back toward the road. As I passed the side of the ravine, I slipped and she tumbled from my arms. It — it was horrible!"

"I didn't cross the line," insisted the other driver. When I heard his car crash through the rail, I braked and hurried back to help."

"What did you see?" asked Haledjian.

"He was carrying the young lady," admitted the second driver. "As he got near the embankment, he slipped to his knees and the girl fell without a sound."

Haledjian descended the treacherously wet embankment. The intermingling of grass, rocks, and mud made a search for footprints useless.

At the spot where the first driver said he lost his hold, Haledjian could see the broken figure of the girl a hundred feet below.

Back on the road he said, "You should hold both these men on suspicion of murder, officer."

Why?

Haledjian suspected that the two men had staged the accident. When the driverless car missed the ravine and crashed into the tree instead, they had thrown the girl to her death.

Had the young man "slipped to his knees" in the mud, as his overeager accomplice claimed, his clothes in that area would not have been "spotless."

The Case of the
Health Formula

Bertie Tilford, the Englishman who had sold the Brooklyn Bridge more often than any man alive, ushered a robust young man into Dr. Haledjian's living room.

"Meet Howard Kent, the physical wonder of the century!" exclaimed Bertie.

Kent dropped to the floor and commenced doing pushups like a trip-hammer. Then he jumped to his feet and began to remove his clothing.

Haledjian barely had time to note that his suit, though it fit well and was neatly pressed, was threadbare. His left shoe had a large hole in the sole.

Stripped, Kent flexed his massive physique in all directions.

"Would you believe that he gained 70 pounds of solid muscle in the past seven months?" asked Bertie. "He's developed a secret, high-protein food formula, which, combined with proper exercise — "

"And you need capital to market the formula," said Haledjian.

"Quite so," sighed Bertie. "Why, the suit Kent's wearing is two years old. He's put every cent into perfecting his secret formula. And I am, frankly, temporarily out of funds, or I should plunge for the whole thing myself.

"All we need is $15,000, dear boy," Bertie ran on. "You'll better mankind and realize a fortune besides!"

"Not today," muttered Haledjian darkly. "You'd have a better chance of selling me the Brooklyn Bridge!"

What was wrong with Bertie's pitch?

Kent's suit, which Bertie claimed was "two years old," still "fit well," though he had supposedly put on 70 pounds "in the past seven months." Impossible!

194

The Case of the
Horseshoe Pitcher

On the day the Carson home was burglarized, the family was away. They had, however, allowed the neighborhood children to play in their large backyard.

The yard was well equipped for children, and encircled by a seven-foot stone wall into which admission was gained by a solid oak door.

Dr. Haledjian entered the yard to call Billy Wills home for supper. Billy and three other boys were pitching horseshoes.

Without arguing, Billy stopped playing. He picked up his baseball glove and accompanied Haledjian home.

"I gotta obey," the boy said. "Tomorrow is my birthday."

At Billy's house, Haledjian saw Mrs. Wills talking with Ed Tate, a neighbor and an ex-convict.

"The game would have been over in a couple more

195

innings," Billy said disappointedly. "Gosh, if I had the right equipment, we could have played here and finished before dinner."

Ed Tate grinned. "Maybe you'll get it for your birthday."

To Billy's mother, Tate said, "Thanks for the loan of the wrenches. I've been fighting the washing machine all day."

The next morning Haledjian read that the Carson home had been robbed. Upon learning that Ed Tate had given Billy Wills a horseshoe pitching set for his birthday, the sleuth advised the police to pick up Tate for questioning.

How come?

Tate's remark about working "all day" was an obvious alibi. As Billy Wills carried a baseball glove and used the word "innings," Tate should have assumed he wanted baseball equipment for his birthday.

Only by being inside the Carson house could Tate have seen Billy pitching horseshoes — a game in which the term "inning" is also used.

The Case of the
Hot Tip

Before Inspector Winters could bellow a protest, Nick the Nose had slipped into his office.

"I got something this time," the little informer insisted. "Last night I'm sleeping in this abandoned warehouse when I hear noises. A voice says, 'Did you glim that piece on page 29 about Mrs. Vandermill?'

"There's a hole in the floor," continued Nick. "I can see four tough eggs sitting in the room below. One of them picks up a newspaper and turns to the back page and starts reading out loud. What he reads goes something like this: 'The Baritoni collection of jewels has been purchased by Mrs. C. Worthington Vandermill of 292 Sea Cliff Heights. Mrs. Vandermill told reporters she will keep the jewels, valued at more than a million dollars, in her house, which she claims is burglar proof.'

"The four guys begin to laugh," Nick went on.

"One guy says, 'Harry, make sure the car is running good, because tomorrow night we're going to pay Mrs. Vandermill a quiet little visit.' "

"There is no Sea Cliff Heights in this city," said Inspector Winters. He lifted a hand.

Nick the Nose remained unshaken. "They were probably reading an out-of-town paper. They'll be back tonight. For ten bucks I'll take you — "

The inspector rose menacingly.

"Five?" yelped Nick.

"Five — fingers," growled the inspector, putting five on Nick's collar and five on the seat of his pants. Haledjian opened the door wide as the little informer flew out into the hall.

Why wasn't Nick paid off?

Although the article on Mrs. Vandermill appeared on page 29, it was read from the "back page." Alas for Nick the Nose, the back page of a newspaper always has an even number.

198

The Case of the
Jade Monkey

"The Staffords were known to be in reduced cir-
cumstances. Owed everybody," said Henderson, the
insurance investigator. "The ten thousand dollars
they'll collect on the shattered art treasure will save
their scalps."

"Then it's your conviction the jade monkey was
deliberately broken?" asked Dr. Haledjian.

"Of course, but I can't budge the eyewitness, Mrs.
Endicott. She's the Staffords' neighbor and closest
friend.

"A few moments before the alleged 'accident,'
Mrs. Endicott received a box containing a mink coat.
It was her first fur, and since it was a warm August
day, she went directly upstairs to unpack and hang
it in the storage closet.

"The window next to the storage closet," continued the insurance man, "is the only one in her house
that has a view into the Staffords' bedroom. After

hanging up the coat, Mrs. Endicott heard Mrs. Stafford scream and saw her neighbor stumble into the jade monkey. It sailed through the open bedroom window and shattered on the patio below.

"The fur company's driver noted the Endicott delivery was made at 3:30 P.M. About a minute later, he heard Mrs. Stafford scream. Rushing from the truck, he saw the fragments of the jade monkey, and both women at their windows."

"As it was a warm August day," interrupted Haledjian, "why wasn't there a screen on the Stafford window?"

"It was being repaired. That was the first angle I investigated. About the only thing I've got to go on is the hunch Mrs. Endicott is lying for her friend."

"I should take the matter to court before paying," agreed Haledjian. "And make sure you have several women on the jury."

What did Haledjian mean by the last remark?

Mrs. Endicott's presence at the *only* window where she could substantiate Mrs. Stafford's claim was obviously part of a plot to collect the insurance money. Haledjian realized other women would instantly see through it.

No woman receiving her first mink would ever put it directly into storage. She would try it on and purr over it.

The Case of the
Lady Larruper

The cab driver sported a shiner three shades of blue, a swollen lip, and a mouthful of missing teeth.

"We found your cab abandoned by Pier 9," said Inspector Winters. "You didn't report it missing, and you weren't at work today. Come on, now. What happened?"

The cabbie, a sizeable young man, looked at the floor. Finally, under the prodding of Inspector Winters and Dr. Haledjian, he shamefacedly detailed the manner of his wounds.

"I picked up this fare on the corner of Madison and 49th," he said. "She was a real big doll with a husky voice. She yanked open the door and gave me an address in the west Bronx, and then climbed in.

"When we reached Riverdale, I swung off the parkway, and she suddenly told me to pull up. It was dark, and the street was one of those private roads with no through traffic.

" 'All right, baby,' she said, 'play it smart and you won't get hurt.'

201

"I slid from behind the wheel and opened the door for her. 'Lady,' I said, 'You shouldn't play like a tough guy. Out!'

"She got out sort of funny. 'Want it the hard way, do you?' she said.

"Pow! She rammed me in the eye with a fist. I went down, surprised. She was big, but not that big.

"She belted me twice more, fast, like a pro, once in the mouth and once in the stomach. When I woke up, my wallet was gone, and so were four teeth and my cab. I was too sick to work today. Holy cats, I never thought a dame could strong-arm me to sleep."

"We have your cab," said Haledjian. "And if we can't recover your wallet, it might comfort you to know that it was undoubtedly a man dressed as a woman who beat you up."

How did Haledjian know?

The "big doll" gave the address, and *then* climbed into the cab.

Haledjian knew what the cabbie should have known: that 90 percent of male riders tell the address before sitting down — while outside the cab, or on the way. And 99 percent of the female passengers never give their destination until *after* they are settled on the seat.

If you're a doubter, ask any big city cabbie.

202

The Case of the
Lincoln Letter

"It might be genuine," murmured Dr. Fry, chief of the crime lab.

Inspector Winters peered through a magnifying glass at the ragged sheet of foolscap. He read the writing, from which part had been torn:

" '. . . in Gettysburg at the Wills home facing the public square. Bands blared, serenading whomever spoke. I begged to be excused. The crowd was little pleased. The band played the national anthem and moved on to Seward's. . . .' "

The last sentence ran into a tear. However, the signature was unmarred — "A. Lincoln."

"It might be worth tens of thousands of dollars," said Dr. Fry.

"For an incomplete letter of President Lincoln's?" inquired the inspector. "Are they that rare?"

"Look at the reverse side," advised Dr. Fry.

The inspector released a low whistle of astonishment. On the other side of the sheet was scrawled a partial draft of the Gettysburg address!

"I found it by accident in the old Bible my sister keeps in the attic," said Sy "The Weasel" McCloskey.

"Wasn't that where you found the counterfeit tens last year?" put in the inspector sarcastically.

Dr. Fry interrupted. "I'll run some chemical tests on the paper. It'll take a couple of days."

"The paper turned out to be the right age," a surprised Inspector Winters reported to Dr. Haledjian. "I'll wager you'll never guess the value of that one little sheet!"

"About 10 cents — to a police museum," replied Haledjian. "It is obviously a forgery."

What was the weasel's error?

The two words, "national anthem."
While *The Star Spangled Banner* was the foremost patriotic song of Lincoln's day, it did not officially become our national anthem until 1931. During his presidency there was no national anthem.

The Case of the
Locked Wine Cellar

Because Wentworth Boyd invariably caught the 9:53 express Friday morning and arrived at his country home exactly two hours later, Dr. Haledjian was able to solve the theft of $50,000 from Boyd's wall safe.

One Friday, Boyd broke his habit without advising anyone. On this day he arrived home shortly before midnight and found his front door ajar. Down in the basement, locked in the wine cellar, he heard his secretary, Nigel Arbuter, shouting for help.

"Coming!" cried Boyd.

"Mr. Boyd!" called Arbuter. "Robbers. I heard them say they'd catch the midnight train back to New York City!"

Boyd freed Arbuter, telephoned the police, and drove to the station. Too late. The train had already pulled out, foiling the police as well.

Dr. Haledjian, at Boyd's request, made his investigation the next day.

"You say two masked robbers forced you at gunpoint to unlock the safe?" he inquired.

"That's right," said Arbuter. "Then they forced a pill — some sort of sleeping potion — down my throat. I awoke in the wine cellar just before Mr. Boyd came downstairs."

Haledjian inspected the wine cellar, a windowless room 13 feet by 9 feet. The door locked from the outside. A single 40-watt bulb cast dim but adequate illumination.

Haledjian looked down at Arbuter's wristwatch. "Were you wearing it at the time of the robbery?"

"Why, y-yes," replied the secretary.

"Then kindly tell us where you hid the money you helped steal!" Haledjian ordered.

What was Arbuter's slip?

As the wine cellar was windowless, Arbuter could not, from his watch, have known how long he'd been unconscious, or whether it was near to the noon or midnight train. Indeed, since Boyd always in the past came home at noon, Arbuter, unless he'd seen Boyd arriving and had his accomplices lock him in, would have supposed it was noon — twelve hours too late to chase the robbers.

The Case of the
Lost Spectacles

"How did you obtain a key to the Carlin home?" demanded Inspector Winters.

"See here," retorted Bartlett, "I've been an old friend of the Carlins for twenty years. I resent your — "

"I've just spoken with John Carlin by long distance," said the inspector evenly. "He claims there was ten thousand dollars in negotiable bonds in his strongbox. There's not ten cents there now. So begin at the beginning."

Bartlett sputtered, and then said: "Carlin asked me to check his house before he returns from Florida on Tuesday. I had intended to drop by tomorrow. I went today instead because it's been below freezing for the past week, and I thought I'd make sure there was enough heat in the house."

Bartlett gazed momentarily at the heavy icicles on the window. "Carlin had mailed a key to me from

207

Miami. As I entered the house about nine this morning, I heard a noise in the study.

" 'Who's there?' I called, and immediately opened the study door. There were two of them. I hadn't a chance once they knocked my spectacles off. I can't see ten feet without them. The pair tied me up, and it wasn't till three hours later that I managed to work free and call the police."

"Could you identify either of the thieves?"

"If I ever saw them again," said Bartlett.

"Did you turn up the heat?"

"Why, no," answered Bartlett hesitantly. "The thermostat was set for 75, and the house was quite warm enough."

In talking to Haledjian the next day, the inspector said, "I'm convinced Bartlett broke into Carlin's strongbox, but I've nothing to hold him on."

"Nothing," asserted Haledjian, "except that he never saw two thieves in the study."

Why not?

Entering a house heated to 75 degrees from the outdoors on a below freezing day, Bartlett could not have seen anything. His glasses would have been steamed over completely.

The Case of the
Lost Stamp

Dr. Haledjian squatted in the sand in front of Murphy's oceanside home and gazed intently at a seagull's footprints that led to the ocean.

"The gull ran across the beach in a takeoff within the past half hour," said Haledjian. "Else, the high tide of half an hour ago would have obliterated its prints."

"Good grief!" said Murphy. "I asked you out here to help me calm down DeCovey when he arrives, not to tell me about seagulls."

"So you said," replied Haledjian sarcastically. "You have the only two existing one-penny Guiani of the 1857 issue. But one stamp blew into the ocean."

"Both stamps were on my desk, ready for DeCovey to examine," said Murphy. "He promised to pay $10,000 for the better one."

"You said the window behind your desk — the

209

one facing the ocean — was open?" inquired Haledjian.

"Yes, a strong wind was blowing from the land all morning. Suddenly the window on that side blew open. In the cross draft, one of the stamps blew off the desk and sailed right into the ocean. I was lucky to save the other!"

"There's not a breath of wind now."

"It stopped dead half an hour ago," said Murphy. "About the time I telephoned you to come over."

"If one of two existing Guianis is worth $10,000, the sole remaining one will be worth at least $20,000 to DeCovey," said Haledjian. "You wanted me to corroborate your story. I won't — because you still have the 'missing' other!"

What made Haledjian so sure?

The seagull's footprints proved the wind blew from the ocean, not from the land. So the stamp could not have been blown into the water. A seagull, like an airplane, takes off against the wind!

The Case of the
Marathon Runner

While motoring through South America, Dr. Haledjian arrived at a forest village half an hour before the start of the annual 26-mile foot race.

Although the race was held as the climax of the harvest festival, a joyous occasion, both villagers and runners seemed blanketed in gloom.

Haledjian asked the race's lone official for the reason.

"The winner," said the official, "used to receive a prize equal to $1,000. When the old landlord died, his son took over, and he entered his own son Juan in the race. Juan has won every year since. Thus the family saves the $1,000.

"Under the new landlord's rules, the runners are timed. They go off separately, one every five minutes, instead of together. Juan always starts first.

"The course goes through the forest there, a hundred yards away, and describes a circle. The

211

runners return up the same path to finish at the starting line.

"I am sure Juan merely runs a hundred yards into the woods, hides, and runs out at the proper time.

"I am the only official. As I come from another village, I do not fear the landlord. I would like to prove Juan cheats, but no one will help me. Here everyone is afraid to complain. If there is no race, the landlord threatened to increase taxes," concluded the official.

"You don't need any help but a tape measure," said Haledjian. "Before the race, measure — "

Measure what?

Measure Juan's calves. And measure them again at the end of the race. After covering 26 miles, a runner's calves will have increased an inch or more.

The Case of the
Million-to-One Shot

"The law of averages will sooner or later produce an extraordinary event," said Dr. Haledjian. "If taken by itself, such an event appears as a phenomenon — the product of wildest chance. Actually, it is but a logical variation from the common mass of nearly similar events."

Haledjian paused to hand Octavia a cup of coffee.

Then he resumed. "An excellent illustration is the disappearance of the bullets in the duel fought by the French twins, Marcel and Henri Laval, in 1857.

"Except that Marcel was left-handed, the twins were so alike that even their parents had difficulty telling them apart.

"Henri and Marcel received excellent military educations, and were soon reputed the best marksmen in the French Army. Inevitably, they fell in love with the same damsel. For young men of honor, one solution only was possible. A duel.

"You may picture it now, after a hundred years. The brothers standing back to back as had hundreds before them; then marching and wheeling at the count like mirror images.

"They fired simultaneously. To the seconds, the shots sounded as one. By a miracle, the brothers weren't scratched, though both confessed to having aimed to kill.

"The pistols were examined and found in perfect working order. Yet neither in the barn behind Marcel, nor the fence behind Henri, was either bullet located.

"The disappearance of the bullets into thin air had a mystic effect on the twins. They resigned their commissions. As the object of the duel ran off with a Hungarian nobleman, they married twin sisters of a merchant of Marseille.

"Now I've given you the clues — the law of averages and the similarity of the twins, Octavia, my dear," concluded Haledjian. "You should have no trouble in determining what really happened to the two bullets."

What?

The bullets fell on the ground between the twin brothers. They had collided and fused in midair!

The Case of the
Missing
Fingerprints

A young farmer, responding to a radio bulletin describing the stolen car used by four masked men in the holdup of the First National Bank, reported that the car had been abandoned near his farm. The four occupants had fled in such haste that they left the four doors wide open.

Shortly after Inspector Winters and Dr. Haledjian reached the scene, another patrol car arrived. Out stepped a hefty man, who said, "I'm Carlson, fingerprints. Headquarters sent me. Can I start?"

The Inspector nodded, and Carlson opened his kit and began dusting the steering wheel of the getaway car.

"It looks like the robbers tried to elude capture by taking the back roads," said the inspector. "They lost their way, ran out of gas, and fled on foot."

More police arrived, and the inspector went off to direct a search of the surrounding area. Haledjian was examining the ground for clues when Carlson finished.

"I've found several prints on the front of the hood and on the gas cap," he said. "They probably belong to the real owner or a gas station attendant. The rest are smudged."

"Too bad," muttered Haledjian. His brows knitted thoughtfully as he watched Carlson open the door of his patrol car and climb in.

Suddenly Haledjian shouted to one of the officers, "Stop that man!"

Why?

Carlson gave himself away by dusting the steering wheel first. A genuine fingerprint expert would have started at the most likely source of clear prints — the front door windows.

Carlson confessed: He had subdued the real fingerprint expert assigned to the case and had taken his place in order to destroy the holdup gang's prints.

The Case of the
Model Universe

"What's it now?" asked Dr. Haledjian. "A uranium mine, sunken bullion, or a pill that converts dishwater into high octane gasoline?"

"Nothing as paltry as that, old chap," answered Bertie Tilford, a young Englishman with more get-rich-quick ideas than fleas on a monkey. "I'm investing in the universe."

Bertie paused to observe the effect of his words. Then he qualified, "Or at least as much of the universe as can be seen by our most powerful telescopes."

Haledjian merely registered skepticism.

"It's the coming thing, the universe," said Bertie. "Five centuries ago man stood on the threshold of vast discoveries. Columbus brought back reports of a new world. Today, man stands on the threshold of thousands of new worlds!"

"You're planning to buy stock," guessed Haledjian. "On Mars or Venus?"

"On this!" exclaimed Bertie. With a regal gesture he produced a tiny ball. It proved to be a beautifully wrought one-half inch model of the earth.

"Professor Stanford T. Platt is going to build a model of the universe, as accurate as modern science allows. We'll show it in stadiums and indoor arenas like Madison Square Garden. It'll be educational!"

"And costly," muttered Haledjian.

"You've got to spend to make," returned Berti. "Professor Platt is trying to raise a million dollars. He'll need to manufacture thousands of stars and planets and moons and what not. But it'll be a sensation. Every schoolchild in America will want to see this exhibit. Every man and woman! I'm going to buy fifty shares at a hundred dollars apiece."

"And lose every penny of it," said Haledjian.

What was wrong with the scheme?

Professor Platt couldn't squeeze his exhibition into Yankee Stadium.

To reproduce even part of the universe in a model scaled down to a half-inch earth would mean that the nearest fixed star must be placed more than 20,000 miles away.

The Case of the
Mugged Secretary

The body of Shirley Tanner, secretary to an airline president, was found in the alley behind the Wright Printers.

Police theorized that she was the victim of a mugger who, growing desperate at her struggles, strangled her. Her pocketbook, emptied of cash, was discovered in a garbage pail at the end of the alley.

Investigation disclosed that around noon on the day of her death, a typed note had been left on the desk of a co-worker, Julie Biers.

Inspector Winters showed Dr. Haledjian the note. It read:

Julie:
I accidently spilled indelible ink on all the stationary in stock. I feel so badly that I'm going to the Wright Printers to have more printed at once. I'll be back at two.
Shirley

"Somebody could have spilled the ink, typed the note, and got Miss Tanner's fingerprints on the sheet — all after she was killed. Somebody," said Haledjian, "who wanted her death to look like the unfortunate outcome of a mugging."

"Miss Tanner could leave her office without being seen," said the inspector thoughtfully. "And the note was left while the other girls were at lunch. But what grounds have you for suspecting a carefully planned, premeditated murder?"

"The faked clue," snapped Haledjian.

What was the clue?

Had Miss Tanner, the secretary to an airline president, written the note, she never would have made three elementary errors.

"Accidently" was written instead of "acciden- tally," "badly" instead of "bad," and "stationary" instead of "stationery."

The Case of the
Murdered Uncle

Eric Armbruster had never left New York City in all his 72 years. What enticed him to the Shelby Arms Hotel in Portland, Oregon, and to his death was a mystery.

There was no mystery about what killed him — a .22 slug above the right ear.

Seated in the office of Inspector Winters in New York City, Dr. Haledjian read the report forwarded by the Portland authorities.

According to the report, the hotel elevator operator remembered taking a middle-aged woman to Armbruster's floor on the night of the murder. He did not take her down again. She had departed, apparently, by the fire stairs.

"Armbruster's next of kin is a niece, Gertrude Armbruster. I expect she'll inherit the bulk of his estate," said the inspector. "I'm going out to tell her of her uncle's death. Hate these jobs. Come along, will you?"

At the niece's apartment, the inspector bowed, mumbled a bit, and finally got out his message.

"I'm sorry I must tell you this. Your Uncle Eric was shot to death in a Portland hotel six hours ago."

The niece, a plump woman of 50, collapsed into a chair and covered her face with her hands.

"Do you know why your uncle made the trip?" asked the inspector.

Gertrude Armbruster shook her head. "No. He doesn't know a soul in Oregon. All his business connections and friends are in New York."

Haledjian glanced at the inspector, who by then was getting ready to make the arrest.

Why?

Although she could not have heard of her uncle's slaying, the niece knew he died in Portland, Oregon. As the state was not told her, she had no way of knowing which of a dozen Portlands was the site of the murder — unless she was involved.

The Case of the
Mysterious Groceries

"A punk who was caught holding up a filling station yesterday has confessed to several unsolved crimes," Inspector Winters told Dr. Haledjian.

"He named Red Kirk as his partner in a supermarket holdup a few years back.

"This morning," went on the inspector, "I picked up a search warrant and visited Kirk's last known address, a boarding house on Waco. Kirk wasn't in, but his roommate, Les Curran, a counterfeiter, showed up at noon. He denied knowing where Kirk was.

"This is the last day of the month. So Kirk, who by the way is a vegetarian, has only to keep moving and stay out of sight for 30 days. In another month the statute of limitations will expire on his supermarket job. He'll be in the clear.

"The part that baffles me is the groceries I found on Kirk's bed," concluded the inspector. I can't fig-

223

ure them. There were six coffee beans, eight boxes of cocoa, 10 tomatoes, four pieces of toast, 14 boxes of hominy, 21 tea bags, and 27 cubes of sugar!"

After a moment's reflection, Haledjian said:

"Kirk plans to keep moving about the country next month to avoid capture, but you should have no trouble apprehending him. The nearest place to find him is — "

Where?

Toast, NC.

Haledjian deduced that the foodstuffs were an itinerary in code for Kirk's roommate, Curran, with the number of each article standing for the day of the month in which Kirk would be at a particular place.

Hence Kirk's itinerary was: Toast, NC; Coffee, GA; Cocoa, FL; Tomato, MS; Hominy, OK; Tea, SD; Sugar, ID.

The Case of the
Olympic Athlete

"I've locked the gates," said the aged caretaker. "Nobody will be able to get in or out of the grounds tonight, Doctor."

Dr. Haledjian nodded approvingly and returned to the mansion of Mildred Emerson. The young heiress had asked him to her house party as a combination guest and protector. In the past week she had received several telephone calls threatening her life.

The most conspicuous of the house guests was the unsteady figure of Biff Walters. The Olympic pole vaulter was rapidly drinking his way out of Mildred's affections.

At midnight, as Haledjian was undressing, he heard Mildred scream, and then the reports of two quick shots. Throwing on a robe, he rushed to her bedroom.

"The jewels — stolen!" she gasped. "The thief tried to kill me!"

"Did you see who it was?" demanded Haledjian.

"No — I didn't see anyone. It all occurred so swiftly. I fainted, and when I came to, my jewel box was gone."

"Was your door locked?"

"Yes. I had to unlock it to admit you," the trembling girl replied. "The thief must have climbed through the window."

"Impossible," said Haledjian, drawing back the curtains. "It's a sheer 15-foot drop to the ground."

Below, Haledjian saw the caretaker playing his flashlight in the flowerbed beneath the window.

"See any ladder marks?" inquired the criminologist.

"Nope. Just a bunch of footprints and a single hole about as big as my wrist and a couple inches deep," was the reply.

"I might have guessed you'd find exactly that," said Haledjian.

Whom did he suspect?

Mildred Emerson — of trying to frame Biff Walters, of whom she was tiring. The imprints in the flowerbed were supposed to indicate Biff had used a pole to climb to her window.

Although the girl had claimed she did not see the thief, she had screamed before the shots were fired.

The Case of the
Petite Wife

"I'll have to take you down to headquarters, Mr. Logan," said Inspector Winters. "Your car was identified as the one seen speeding away from the corner of Everett and Rose, where the Burton boy was hit this morning."

"Obviously, there's been a mistake," said Logan, a huge man of six feet six inches. "I haven't driven the car in two days."

"Larry Appleson, a playmate of the injured boy, is pretty sure it was your car, and driven by a big man," replied the inspector.

Logan laughed genially. "Now I know there's been an error. The only person who drove the car this morning was my wife. She hardly can be mistaken for a man."

The inspector glanced at Mrs. Logan, a pale blonde, hardly five feet tall.

"I put it to you, inspector," said Logan. "Could you mistake Claire for a man?"

"No," agreed the inspector. "One other thing. The hit-run car made a lot of noise, as if it had muffler trouble."

"Listen for yourself," invited Logan, leading the inspector to the garage.

Taking a set of keys from his pocket, he slipped comfortably behind the wheel, and started the motor without delay. He backed the car onto the street and drove twice around the block.

"The car operated noiselessly," the inspector told Haledjian later. "But even before I discovered it had a new muffler, I knew Logan was lying."

Haledjian knew, too. Did you?

Although Logan claimed his five-foot wife was the only person to drive the car that morning, he was able to slip "comfortably behind the wheel." Since he was six and a half feet tall, he would have had to adjust the seat from her position to his if she had really been the last driver.

The Case of the
Phony Fight

"A woman's mind is the one insoluble mystery," admitted Dr. Haledjian to the thin, bespectacled youth. "But I'll help you if I can."

Cyril Makin nodded gratefully, cleared his throat, and said, "I'd been secretly in love with Gladys Brewster for two years. My chances seemed hopeless. She's one of those big outdoorsy girls, a champion skier and swimmer. I never did better than assistant manager of the high school basketball team. Can't see twenty feet without my glasses.

"I knew she'd never take me seriously unless I proved myself a man. So I enlisted the aid of Rocky Armstrong, the heavyweight boxing champion.

"He had staged private 'fights' before, I was relieved to learn. Even had a straight fee for getting knocked down. Two thousand dollars, in advance. A lot of money, but I paid.

"The next night I escorted Gladys to Rocky's

Steak House on 12th Street. The place was crowded as usual, and we were asked to wait in a small anteroom by ourselves.

"Presently Rocky entered, eyed Gladys up and down, and made an improper remark. I demanded a retraction. He laughed at me.

" 'I don't like to do this,' I said and, slipping my glasses into my breast pocket, threw up my fists and went for him.

"Glady screamed. Rocky waded in, pounded me unmercifully about the body. I pressed on, undaunted. A smart left to the jaw laid him down and out, just as we'd rehearsed it.

" 'Let's get out of here,' I snapped, replacing my glasses and grabbing Gladys. She looked at me mutely, sheer worship shining in her eyes.

"It was in the taxicab that the look changed. 'You staged the fight!' she cried. 'You phony!'

"I've called her countless times since, but she won't speak with me. How the dickens did she know the fight was faked?"

Haledjian knew. Do you?

Gladys knew the champ had pulled his punches: Although he had pounded Cyril "unmercifully about the body," Cyril had removed his eyeglasses from his breast pocket after the fight — *unbroken.*

230

The Case of the
Pirated Yacht

On a clear summer night five armed men in a power skiff chugged alongside the yacht *Coral Reef*.

Too big to be tied up at the Wilson Yacht Club piers, the yacht lay at anchorage in deeper waters. The five armed men boarded her, put the captain and his crew of three into the skiff, and headed the *Coral Reef* out to sea.

No word of her was had for a month.

"The night she was pirated," Inspector Winters told Dr. Haledjian, "the *Coral Reef* carried a cargo destined for Italy — medicines worth millions."

"I never believed the story the captain and his crew told about being surprised," said Haledjian. "I take it you have news?"

"This morning I received a telegram from a federal agent," said the inspector. "He reports the *Coral Reef* is at Anchorage, Alaska, abandoned and empty."

The telephone on the inspector's desk rang.

"That must be the captain of the *Coral Reef*. I placed a call to him in Chicago," said the inspector.

He picked up the receiver and spoke. "Captain Shea? I have good news. The *Coral Reef* is at Anchorage. You will? Fine."

Hanging up, the inspector said, "The captain said he'll notify the owners at once. Then he'll fly to Alaska and take possession of the yacht if he is able to."

"But he won't be able to," said Haledjian, grinning. "You'll have him under arrest for piracy within the hour!"

Why?

Over the telephone the inspector had simply said the yacht was "at Anchorage."

Had the captain truly been an innocent victim of the piracy, he should have heard "at anchorage," and asked, "Where?"

Instead, he knew immediately she was at the port, Anchorage, in Alaska.

232

The Case of the
Poisoned Mice

A bright glitter of reminiscence came to Dr. Haledjian's eye when Octavia, his fair dinner companion, ordered a cheese-and-celery soufflé.

"I am reminded of a mice poisoning case in England many years ago," he said.

"Mice?" squeaked Octavia. "Don't tell me! You'll
ruin my appetite!"

Haledjian ignored the protest.

"I had gone to visit the Mousery of Freddie Monte-
Culver outside London," began the sleuth. "It was
a time when mouse shows were the craze. A prize
mouse was not only colored black and white, but
blue, red, chocolate, lilac, and even champagne.

"Freddie wasn't in, but Reeves, his assistant, a
genial fellow in a tight-fitting white lab coat, showed
me around.

" 'A perfect mouse should have a tail the same
length as the body,' he explained, slipping a stud

233

mouse a bit of cheese. 'A superbly or uniquely colored specimen can be sold for as much as £750.'

"The next day I telephoned Freddie as I was departing for the Continent. I learned to my dismay — but hardly to my surprise — that many of his best mice had died mysteriously.

" 'Fire your assistant,' I advised."

How come?

Haledjian knew that Reeves was feeding the mice cheese, which poisoned them.

A thousand white mice and more can be fed oats, milk, bread, and raw eggs inexpensively and safely — but never cheese. Cheese overheats their blood!

The Case of the
Power Failure

Turner opened the refrigerator in his mountain cabin and withdrew an ice tray. By the candlelight, Dr. Haledjian could see his hands were trembling as he deposited three cubes into a highball glass.

Haledjian could hardly blame the young novelist for trembling. They had just come from the den, where Turner's housekeeper, Lucy, lay dead of a broken neck.

"I thought she was a burglar," exclaimed Turner, downing his drink.

"After the generator failed four days ago," he continued, "I lost all electrical power up here. I'd rented the cabin to be alone in order to put a high polish on my latest novel. I like to work at night, but not without lights. So I moved to a motel in town.

"Two hours ago — a little after midnight — I came back here to get some notes. I'd put down my flashlight to unlock a desk drawer when Lucy jumped me from behind. I guess she thought I was a burglar.

"She's trained in judo, and in the dark I thought I was being attacked by a man. I hit her — and you saw what happened. She fell against the fireplace and broke her neck.

"I heard you were in town, and I fetched you immediately," concluded Turner.

"Why?" demanded Haledjian. "You knew your housekeeper was dead. And if you brought me up here for the purpose of testing your story, I suggest you improve it before the police question you!"

How come?

Turner claimed that he had been without electrical power for "four days," and in the darkness he mistook his housekeeper for a burglar.

However, had he really been without power for four days, the ice cubes in the refrigerator would have turned to water!

The Case of the
Provoked Assault

"You put Everet Evans in the hospital with a broken jaw, but he isn't going to charge you with assault," said Dr. Haledjian. "Mind telling me what this is all about?"

"Evans," answered John Wilmot, "is a gambler and a scoundrel. I've forbidden my son Cliff to associate with him, though Cliff worships the blackguard.

"Three days ago Cliff went to Calred City to visit an aunt for the day, and yesterday I received an anonymous telephone call.

"The caller swore that Cliff had gone with Evans to his hunting lodge, which is five miles from Calred City.

"An hour after the call, I had lunch with Evans and innocently asked him to have me up to the lodge for a weekend of hunting. He was reluctant, said the lodge hadn't been used for months, but he finally consented.

"Upon reaching the lodge, we immediately went out to hunt. We shot two rabbits, and while Evans prepared the game, I looked around.

"It's hard to tell whether a place has been occupied recently, especially if care is taken to cover up. Evans observed my guarded snooping with a supercilious air.

"The lodge was well provisioned with food and drink. We ate the rabbits and some canned fruit. I was just taking a swallow of sweet cider from a half-filled jug — Evans drank Irish whiskey — when he said:

" 'I know what you're really hunting for up here, John.'

"That's when I hit him and broke his jaw," concluded Wilmot.

"I don't condone violence," said Haledjian. "Still, I can readily understand why Evans isn't taking you to court."

Why not?

Evans lied when he said "the lodge hasn't been used for months," since John Wilmot drank "sweet cider from a half-filled jug."

Had the cider been standing in the jug for months, it would have fermented and tasted sour.

The Case of the
Purse Snatcher

Dr. Haledjian was in Inspector Winters' office when Bumbles Brasoon, the nation's most inexpert petty crook, was brought in for questioning.

"The charge is purse snatching outside the new theater on Washington Avenue," snapped the inspector.

"It's a case of mistaken identity!" wailed Bumbles.

"The complainant, Mrs. Ruth Fogerty, didn't give you her pocketbook, now did she?" chided the inspector.

"No, but the real crook did," said Bumbles. "I'll tell you what happened, and it's the truth. I swear on my wife's honor!

"I was walking past the theater thinking about looking for a job when the weather improves. Suddenly I hear a woman scream. This big kid with long hair comes hot-footing past me, carrying a pocketbook.

"He ducks into the alley behind the theater. I give chase like a good citizen. He gets to the theater's fire exit door when he spots me.

"He knows I've got him. So he chucks me the pocketbook, pushes open the door, and slips inside. I'm holding the pocketbook when this rhino of a dame comes charging up the alley with a cop," concluded Bumbles. "I'm innocent!"

After Bumbles had been ushered out, the inspector said to Haledjian, "Mrs. Fogerty isn't certain who snatched her pocketbook. Bumbles' story is weak, but it might be true."

"His story is impossible," said Haledjian.
Why?

The "kid" would have had to enter the theater by pulling open the fire exit door, not by pushing it, as Bumbles claimed.
Theater fire exit doors open out into the street.

The Case of the
Racetrack Murder

The blonde stumbled from the stall shouting, "Please, somebody, in there!"

Dr. Haledjian, who was watching the horses in their early morning workouts, hurried into the stall from which the excited girl had dashed.

Beside a large bay mare, a man attired in horseman's garb lay face down in the straw. An ice pick jutted from a large irregular bloodstain on his lower back.

"Dead about eight hours," muttered Haledjian. "That puts the time of the murder about midnight. Pardon me, isn't that blood on the back of your sleeve, miss?"

The blonde pulled the sleeve of her stylish riding habit around and peered at a long smear of blood on the underside.

"Oh," she gasped faintly. "I must have brushed

against the wound when I stooped over him just before."

When the police arrived, she said, "I'm Gale Devore, Th-that's Pete Murphy, who trains my mare, Black Bay."

Haledjian asked, "Do you know anyone who had reason to kill Murphy?"

"No," the girl answered. "Except, perhaps . . . Bob Ford. Pete owed him a great deal of money. . . ."

"Fifteen thousand dollars, to be exact," the inspector told Haledjian the next morning. "But Ford, who runs a fish store, swears he hasn't been near Miss Devore's stable for two days. Incidentally, the blood on her sleeve is the same type as the dead man's."

"You made an arrest, I take it?" said Haledjian.

"The suspect is in jail right now," replied the inspector.

Who is the suspect?

Gale Devore, who lied in claiming she got the blood on her sleeve when she "brushed against the wound when I stooped over him just before." As Murphy was dead eight hours by then, his blood would have been too dry to smear her sleeve.

242

The Case of the
Railroad Robbery

"What time will we arrive in San Francisco?" asked Dr. Haledjian, as the conductor passed his seat in the Pullman.

"In exactly one hour — at twenty minutes after three," was the reply. "Your first trip to California?"

"No, but my first time to the northern part of the state," replied the famed sleuth.

"Well, you'll like 'Frisco," said the conductor genially. "Great town. Been living there myself for thirty-two — "

Just then a blond young man charged down the aisle shouting, "In compartment 6! Come at once!"

With the blond leading, the conductor and Haledjian rushed to the car directly behind them. A white-haired man was slumped in the seat of compartment 6. He had been knocked unconscious.

"It's Harry Winslow, the New York jeweler," said Haledjian. "He's a bit of a showman — sometimes carries a million dollars in jewels with him and makes no secret of it."

"Looks like you've hit the motive," said the conductor, stooping. He picked up an empty jewel case from the floor.

Then he turned sharply to the blond young man. "Who are you and what were you doing in this compartment?"

"My name is Clarence Swezy. My compartment is right next door," answered the young man. "I met Mr. Winslow in the dining car and he invited me in for a drink before we arrived in San Francisco."

The jeweler opened his eyes and put his hand to the bump on the back of his head. "W-what — who hit me?" he groaned.

"He did," snapped Haledjian, and with a deft judo hold he rendered powerless the man he suspected of the jewelry theft.

Which man?

The conductor, whom Haledjian suspected of being an impostor for two reasons.

First, no railroad man would have said "twenty minutes after three," but "three-twenty," in giving the time.

Second, a resident of San Francisco would refer to the city by its full name, and never, never as "Frisco."

The Case of the
Reversed Faucets

Dr. Haledjian was strolling past the small house of Thomas Fremont when the back door swung open violently.

A tall man rushed out. "Dr. Haledjian!" he cried. "Come inside! Something dreadful has happened!"

Haledjian recognized Fremont's prodigal nephew Scott. Hastening inside, he found Fremont lying in the living room on his right side, beyond help. His right hand, covered with blood, fumbled at the handle of the knife protruding from his stomach.

"W-water," Fremont gasped.

Scott seemed rooted to the spot. Haledjian dashed into the kitchen, where he encountered difficulty with the faucets. When at last he filled a glass, Fremont was dead.

"Strange that your uncle asked for water," Haledjian said to Scott after the police arrived. "Another thing. The hot and cold faucets in the kitchen are reversed. I turned on the right-hand one and immediately got a jet of hot water. The cold water faucet is on the left."

"Uncle was left-handed," explained Scott. "He had all the faucets in the house reversed. He was a bit of an eccentric — lived here alone for years."

"Had you been inside long before you encountered me?"

"No — I had just arrived. I found him stabbed and ran for help."

"Or tried to escape," snapped Haledjian.

Why did Haledjian doubt Scott?

Fremont's gasp for water was intended to lead Haledjian to his murderer — Scott.

It takes a few moments for hot water to come through the pipes, and the fact that one faucet "immediately" gave "a jet of hot water" proved it had been used very recently.

Scott confessed. He had washed the blood from his hands before running from the house.

The Case of the
Screaming Cat

"One of your neighbors reported hearing a scream from this house about ten minutes ago," Inspector Winter said. "I'm sorry to intrude, but we happened to be driving nearby, and I thought I'd check on the report myself."

James McNalty stood scowling in the doorway — till he saw the inspector's badge. "There's some mistake," he protested. "B-but come in."

The inspector and Dr. Haledjian left the rain, which had been falling for three hours, and entered the bright and cheerful little house.

"I'll bet Mrs. Hatfield reported the scream," said McNalty. "She lives next door with her cats. I found a gray one camped at my door when I came home ten minutes ago.

"I was tired and wet and impatient," continued McNalty. "The cat didn't move, so I kicked it —

harder than I intended. It let out a yowl. A yowl, inspector. Not a scream."

"Is that your station wagon in the back?" inquired Haledjian.

"Yes. I've been away selling for two weeks," said McNalty.

Haledjian peered through the window at the station wagon a moment and suddenly went outside.

"Here, pussy," he murmured gently at the gray cat cowering under the station wagon. He moved one hand along the dry gravel beneath the car and then with a lightning motion seized the cat. Carrying it back into the house, he asked McNalty, "Do you live here alone?"

"With my wife, Mae," was the nervous reply.

"For your sake, I hope she's well," said Haledjian. "If there was a scream, I don't think the cat made it!"

What aroused Haledjian's suspicion?

Had McNalty really come home "ten minutes ago," the gravel under his car would have been wet. Instead it was dry, proving the car had been there before the rain started "three hours" before.

Haledjian believed McNalty had spied the cat under the car and used it as an alibi for the scream.

The Case of the
Second Will

"Young Mark Rall insists he found this in an Old Testament in his uncle's library," said Evans, the attorney. He handed Dr. Haledjian a document as both men sat in the criminologist's study.

Haledjian released a low whistle. The document was a last will and testament. It bequeathed the bulk of Arthur Marx Colby's millions to his 22-year-old nephew, Mark Rall.

"This will is either genuine or a dashedly clever forgery," opined Haledjian. "When did Colby die?"

"Last April — April 21, to be exact," answered Evans. "If this will is genuine, it will mean Colby's two elderly sisters, my clients, will be out a fortune."

"I assume this new will is dated after the one leaving the fortune to your clients?"

"Yes, twelve days later," said Evans.

"When did young Rall find it?"

"Last week," said Evans. "He says he had opened

a copy of the Old Testament and there between pages 157 and 158 was this will."

"He's pretty sure of himself," muttered Haledjian.

"He takes pride in a punctilious mind, the young scoundrel," returned Evans. "He's willing to settle out of court — for half his uncle's estate! But I must give him an answer within two hours. Can you spot anything wrong with the will he claims to have found?"

"I'm no expert in the field," concluded the sleuth. "Nevertheless, I should tell young Rall to put this will back where he found it!"

How come?

Rall could not have found the will between pages 157 and 158 as he claimed. Try putting a piece of paper between those pages in the book nearest you!

The Case of the
Silk Mantle

Police established the following facts:

1. On a beastly hot day, a masked man had entered the Cartonses' apartment. In attempting to beat from Mrs. Carton the hiding place of her diamond necklace, he had accidentally killed her. He had ransacked the apartment and fled empty-handed.

2. Mr. Carton, an invalid who had been under sedation during the crime, discovered the body and notified police.

3. Suspicion fell upon Bill, the doorman and an ex-con, who had not reported to work since the slaying.

4. The necklace was safely hidden in the false bottom of a jewelry box in the guest closet near the fireplace. The box rested on the closet shelf above the spot where Mrs. Carton habitually hung her gold silk mantle. She wore this garment in the apartment on chilly days, but never outside the apartment.

Upon ascertaining these facts, Dr. Haledjian asked to be left alone in the apartment with the doorman.

After hearing Bill insist he had never set foot in the apartment, Haledjian shifted a cigarette container and two statuettes on the shelf above the fireplace and rested his elbow there.

"The necklace was right here in the false bottom of a box above the mantle. See for yourself," urged the sleuth. "Come on!"

In a moment, Bill had found the jade box above Mrs. Carton's silk mantle.

After he was clapped under arrest, Haledjian told Inspector Winters, "A criminal should never return to the scene of his crime."

What was Bill's mistake?

Bill insisted he "had never set foot in the apartment," before, yet he knew about the silk mantle in the closet.

An innocent man would have assumed that the necklace was hidden in the cigarette box on the fireplace shelf, or "mantel."

The Case of the
Sleeping Deer

When Dr. Haledjian reached the scene of the fatal hunting accident, he found Sheriff Monahan already there.

"The dead man is H. Harey Morton," said the sheriff. "He and his law partner, Bill Johnson, had been afield two hours when the tragedy struck. Johnson states he missed a shot at a buck, and the bullet pierced Morton's left temple."

Haledjian stooped by the body, which lay face downward, about ten feet from a low thicket. One hand still clutched a rifle. The wound, though messy, was clearly visible, as Morton was hatless.

"I guess I was overanxious," Johnson said remorsefully. "Harvey and I hunted together last year, and we bagged our limit by the second day. But we'd gone four days without a shot before we spotted this big buck.

"He was lying asleep in that little thicket," continued Johnson. "It was Harvey's turn — we always agree on who shoots first. I sneaked in closer, believing Harvey was right behind me. But he must have crept in on the far side of the thicket.

"Well, the buck sensed us, because he suddenly rose to his forelegs. Then his rump came up, and Harvey still didn't fire. The buck was ready to bolt, and I knew I'd have to shoot first or lose the big fellow. I missed — and hit poor Harvey."

"Didn't Harvey wear a red hunting cap?" asked Haledjian.

Johnson looked surprised. "Yes . . . He must have lost it in the woods someplace."

Thanking the distraught hunter, Haledjian returned to the sheriff. "I'd check into the firm of Morton and Johnson," he advised. "I've a strong suspicion Johnson had good reason to kill his partner."

Why did Haledjian suspect Johnson?

Johnson's story was clearly an invention. He said the buck rose first on his forelegs. Unfortunately for him, a deer gets off the ground hind-end first.

The Case of the
Slip of Paper

The night clerk in the Jade Motel was the lone witness to the telephone booth slaying of gambler Ken Cobham.

He told police that Cobham had just spun the dial two or three times when a masked gunman shot Cobham twice in cold blood. The killer escaped as Cobham staggered around a corner and fell dead.

"It's a professional job. No clues. Tomorrow I ought to get a visit from Nick the Nose," sighed Inspector Winters.

Sure enough, the following day as the inspector and Dr. Haledjian, the famed criminologist, were going out to lunch, Nick presented himself at headquarters.

"I got a lead on the Cobham murder," the greasy little informer said.

"You haven't had a lead since you won the sack race in second grade," snapped the inspector.

Unruffled by such heartless truth, Nick handed the inspector a torn slip of paper on which was written "Ze-2-"

"You remember Cobham staggered out of the telephone booth?" asked Nick. "He turned a corner and the night clerk lost sight of him for a few seconds?"

"Yeah, the newspapers had that," said the inspector.

"Cobham bumped into Icky Francisco," said Nick. "Cobham dropped a piece of paper. Icky picked it up. The numbers on that paper are part of a telephone number Cobham must have been calling when he was shot. I got the other half of the paper — with the last four numbers — in my pocket. I figure it's worth something big!"

"How's a size 12?" roared the inspector, and planted his foot persuasively on the seat of Nick's pants.

Why did Nick get the boot?

Cobham, who had "just spun the dial two or three times" when he was shot, could not have been dialing a "Ze" number because there is no Z on the dial. Z is a mobile exchange number, and to be connected the caller must dial operator.

256

The Case of the
Speeding Train

The fat man lay by the railroad embankment, his twisted limbs testifying to the imprudence of leaving a train as it raced at 100 miles per hour.

"Broken neck — probably died instantly," said Dr. Haledjian after a summary examination. "Who is he?"

"Tommy Harner, the New York racketeer," replied Sheriff Monahan. "He must have jumped from the Rocket. It leaves New York for Los Angeles on Tuesday night and passes through here around four Wednesday afternoon. It's the only train by, today."

"What makes you sure Harner jumped?" asked Haledjian.

"For one thing, the money in his wallet. For another, his valises."

"Valises?"

"I'll show you," said the sheriff, shading his eyes

as he led the way down the tracks toward the setting sun.

After some five hundred yards, the two men came to the first valise. It contained expensive clothes monogrammed TH.

Another two hundred yards farther along lay the second valise. It contained fifty thousand dollars in new twenty-dollar bills.

"Counterfeit," said the sheriff. "Apparently someone wanted it, and Harner decided to jump rather than give it up."

"At least that's what someone wants the authorities to believe," said Haledjian. "The killer went to a lot of trouble, but the autopsy will show Harner was slain and then thrown from the train."

How did Haledjian know?

The two valises were found far to the west of the body ("toward the setting sun"), in the same direction as the train traveled (New York to Los Angeles).

Hence, Harner had left the speeding train first and his bags had followed him several seconds later.

The Case of the
Spilled Brandy

In pouring Dr. Haledjian's 20-year-old brandy, Inspector Winters inadvertently spilled a liberal quantity on the carpet. He apologized and chuckled reminiscently. "Last year I arrested a man after he'd spilled some brandy — and not nearly such good stuff as this, either."

"So?" said Haledjian inquiringly.

"I was driving upstate for the weekend," recalled the inspector. "Somehow, I took a wrong turn. I pulled up to a big farmhouse to ask directions.

"As I stopped my car behind a black convertible in the driveway, a young man burst out of the house.

" 'Do you live here?' he shouted excitedly.

"I told him I didn't. Nonetheless he seemed awfully glad to have somebody else around. He said he was a stranger who'd stopped to ask directions a minute before I arrived.

" 'The house is empty — except for a woman lying on the sofa. I th-think she's dead!' he exclaimed.

"The woman wasn't dead, but she wasn't very alive. Not with her head bloody and bruises on her throat. I told the excited young man to find some brandy, and he disappeared into the kitchen while I telephoned the police.

"When the young man came back, I tried to tell him the brandy was to steady his nerves. But he acted too swiftly. He put the bottle to the unconscious woman's lips. He'd spilled most of it over her chin and throat before I yanked the bottle away.

" 'Leave her alone!' I ordered. And just to make it emphatic, I held my gun on him till the local police could place him under arrest. Luckily, the girl survived. But if I hadn't driven up unexpectedly, he'd have finished choking her to death."

How did the inspector know?

The young man claimed to be a stranger in the big farmhouse. Yet he knew the brandy was kept in the kitchen.

The Case of the
Stolen Bible

Dr. Haledjian put the telephone receiver to his ear and heard the frantic voice of Ted Petrie, a rare-book collector.

"A thief took the hinges off the door of one of my book cabinets and made off with a 16th-century Bible," explained Petrie. "Can you come right over to my place?"

Half an hour later, Haledjian stood on the second floor of Petrie's home and examined the small, empty book cabinet. The glass door, unhinged, lay on the carpet.

"I was downstairs watching television," said Petrie. "I went to the kitchen for a bite to eat and suddenly a man dashed down the stairs and out the front door. He was carrying a Bible.

"Of course I chased him. At the corner of Vine and Davis, I lost him in the crowd watching the St.

Patrick's Day parade. I stopped at the first pay telephone and called you.

"I always keep the cabinet locked. I expect the noise of the television kept me from hearing the thief at work upstairs."

"The Bible is insured?" asked Haledjian.

"Yes, for a fortune," answered Petrie. "But money can't replace such a book!"

"Then I suggest you put it back," said Haledjian. "I don't believe a word of your story!"

Why not?

At the time he telephoned Haledjian, Petrie had no way of knowing exactly how the cabinet on the second floor had been opened.

The Case of the
Stolen Painting

Dr. Haledjian arrived ten minutes early for his dinner appointment with Arthur Corning. The evening was to be a celebration. Arthur had just been bequeathed a brownstone house by his cousin, Harriet Trease.

The youth was far from the prototype of the happy heir as he greeted Haledjian.

"Good heavens, if you'd only got here five minutes sooner!" he exclaimed. "The paintings. They've been stolen!"

"Calm yourself and tell me what happened," said Haledjian.

"As you know, my cousin had assembled a modest art collection," said the young man. "Her six favorite oils hung in her study — two by Picasso, two by Renoir, and one each by Turner and Constable. The second-rate works of first-rate artists.

"Ten minutes ago I was alone in the study," went

on the youth. "The burglar came up behind me, announced he had a gun, and ordered me to face the wall by the Renoir.

"He took down the five pictures and told me to hand him the Renoir. Then he slipped out."

"Without your seeing his face," said Haledjian skeptically.

"Wrong," Arthur snapped. "I saw him in the reflection of the glass over the Renoir. I can identify him, and I shall!"

"The pictures were insured?"

"Yes. I don't stand to lose anything, luckily."

"You mean you stand to pocket a tidy sum and still keep the paintings," said Haledjian. "You invited me here to test your story before applying for the insurance, didn't you?"

What was the flaw in Arthur's story?

Arthur lied when he said he saw the burglar's face "in the reflection of the glass over the Renoir." All the stolen paintings were oils, and oils are never framed under glass.

The Case of the
Tardy Witness

"The fight happened last May 30th, and it's just now coming up on the court calendar," said Kronke, the attorney for young Arthur Monroe. "Frankly, I didn't give my client much of a chance. A neighbor who saw the whole thing said Arthur struck Mr. Gilman first."

"What's changed your attitude suddenly?" asked Dr. Haledjian.

"A new witness, John Craft, turned up yesterday. He's a close buddy of Arthur's and claims to have seen the fight from the bank directly across the street. His version is that Mr. Gilman hit Arthur first. I want you to check his story before I put him on the stand."

Haledjian consented. John Craft was ushered in and related what he had seen.

"I'd gone into the First National Bank, but it was lunchtime, and there were long lines in front of all the clerks. I didn't feel like waiting, so I left.

"As I got to the door I had a perfect view of Arthur

and Old Man Gilman approaching each other on the opposite sidewalk. Arthur told me how Old Man Gilman was always needling him. He said if Gilman ever started something, why he'd just walk away.

"Old Man Gilman wouldn't let him walk away. He blocked Arthur and punched him twice in the jaw. Arthur reached up to ward off another blow. Old Man Gilman tripped and hit his neck against Arthur's raised hand.

"That's when the neighbor looked out. She saw Old Man Gilman stagger and fall to the pavement on his face. I guess he got the brain concussion from falling so hard."

"Why didn't you speak up at the time, instead of letting months pass?" asked Haledjian.

"I — I didn't want to get involved," stammered Craft. "I've done time in a reformatory."

"And you'll do more time for perjury if you ever repeat that story under oath," said Haledjian harshly.

What was Craft's lie?

Craft couldn't have been coming from the bank opposite the scene of the fight. The fight occurred on May 30th, Decoration Day, when all banks are closed.

The Case of the
Theft at the Circus

Willie the clown, still attired in his comic knight suit of pots and pans, clanked and clattered to a pile of folded chairs and sat down disconsolately.

"It's true I passed Princess Minerva's trailer five minutes ago. But I didn't steal her money!"

"I saw him slip out of the trailer," insisted Kathy Winslow, an aerial ballerina. "He looked around, stuck a bag under his arm, and hurried off. I couldn't mistake him in that get-up!"

"Come, now, Kathy. You're overwrought," said Princess Minerva, the circus's trapeze star. "Everyone knows where I keep my cash. Why would Willie rob me? We've been together with the circus for twenty years!"

"Calm yourself," cautioned Dr. Haledjian as he finished bandaging Princess Minerva's head. "You're going to be out of action a couple of days."

"Never mind me," said Princess. "Find the thief.

I was sitting with my back to the door reading. I never heard the louse sneak in. What did he hit me with?"

"This," answered Haledjian, holding up a battered pot.

"It's not mine!" protested the clown.

"Don't believe him," said Kathy.

Haledjian studied Willie. His eyes narrowed.

"Your attempt to frame Willie is contemptible," he said to Kathy.

How did Haledjian know?

Princess Minerva said she had not heard the thief enter her trailer. That ruled out Willie in his clanking and clattering knight's rig.

When confronted with this inconsistency, Kathy confessed to the robbery.

The Case of the
13 Roses

The single window and door of Wayne Hector's rented room were both locked from the inside. Police officers, acting on a tip, broke in and found the 40-year-old librarian on the bed, dead of a gunshot wound.

"The flower vendor at the 103rd Street subway station called us this morning," Inspector Winters told Dr. Haledjian over the telephone.

"You see, every Friday evening for ten years Hector bought 13 coral roses. Yesterday he missed his regular stop, and the vendor became worried.

"The way it looks," went on the inspector, "Hector locked the door and window and shot himself while sitting on the bed. He fell over on his right side, dropping the pistol to the carpet. The door key was in his vest pocket."

"What about the roses he bought the previous week?"

"They were wilted and dead in a vase of water on the windowsill," said the inspector. "Hector died about five days ago."

"Does the carpet cover the entire floor?"

"Yes, to about an inch of the walls," replied the inspector.

"Are there any blood stains on the floor, windowsill, or carpet?"

"No, nothing except a little dust. Only on the bed are there bloodstains."

"In that case," said Haledjian, "you had better request laboratory tests of the carpet for bloodstains," said Haledjian. "Somebody with a key to Hector's room killed him as he stood by the window. Then the murderer cleaned up where Hector fell and arranged the body on the bed to make death look like suicide."

How did Haledjian know?

The dead roses on the window sill, after two weeks in the room, should have cast petals on the carpet. Yet the area around the flowers showed "nothing except a little dust."

Haledjian deduced that the petals had been thoughtlessly picked up by the murderer cleaning up the blood.

270

The Case of the
Three Cucumbers

Dr. Haledjian stopped at the street peddler's vegetable stand on the corner of Worth and Station Streets.

"Three cucumbers, please," he said. "Nice ones."

The youthful peddler selected three cucumbers and dropped them into a brown paper bag.

"Three nice ripe ones, mister," he said, handing the famous sleuth the bag and his change.

Opening the bag, Haledjian checked the three green, rough-skinned vegetables, and bumped into a heavy woman carrying a shoulder-strap pocketbook.

He had barely muttered his apologies when a black car turned the corner. It moved slowly toward the entrance of the National Trust Company Bank on the opposite side of the street.

Haledjian glanced quickly up and down the block. Besides the heavy woman and the fruit peddler, two other persons were outdoors.

A tall, natty man was adjusting and readjusting his tie in the reflection of a shoe store window. He seemed dissatisfied with his improvements and repeated them over and over.

Near the bank door, an elderly woman was nervously turning the pages of a bank deposit book.

Haledjian had no chance to intercept the robbers who, a moment later, dashed from the bank and escaped in the black car.

But he did apprehend the gang's lookout.

Whom did he apprehend?

The vegetable peddler, an obvious phony, who called the green cucumbers "ripe." Ripe cucumbers are yellow.

The Case of the
Timely Neigh

The radio newscast carried a report of the death of writer Bill Quist near Strandville. According to the report, Quist had swerved his sports car from his lane and crashed head-on with a green sedan driven by R.J. Phelps, who escaped with a broken arm and lacerations. Both cars tumbled off the road after colliding.

Dr. Haledjian quickly put through a telephone call to the Strandville police. "I've known Bill Quist for years," he told the police chief. "I can't believe he was at fault and I'd like a chance to clear his name."

The chief's tone was snappish. "Quist was to blame, and that's certain. The accident occurred on the hairpin turn due west of the Fleetwood Riding Academy. Ted Dennison, the riding master, saw the whole thing."

Despite the chief's resentment of big-city snoopers, Haledjian drove up to Strandville. A half hour of questioning established that not only was the injured man, R.J. Phelps, a local bigwig, but also the brother-in-law of the only eye-witness to the accident, Ted Dennison. Haledjian spoke with Dennison late in the afternoon.

"I saw it plainly," said the riding master. "I was just mounting Nelly Bly — that little chestnut mare there."

"What made you glance toward the road?"

"She did," said Dennison with a smirk. "I'd got one foot in the stirrup when all of a sudden she neighed, turned her head to the left, and looked at the road almost expectantly. Over her back I saw the two cars — that fellow Quist jumped the center line."

"Why weren't any tire marks found on the road?"

"The fact is," answered Dennison, "the rain washed away all the marks."

"The fact is," retorted Haledjian, "you never saw the accident."

What was the basis for Haledjian's accusation?

The Case of the
Treasure Map

"I asked you over to settle an ugly dispute between my two sons," John Boyd told Dr. Haledjian.

"The affair is this. Last month Carl and Eddie rented a luxury sailboat and cruised the Keys. On one of the islands Carl found a piece of cloth with geographic markings.

"It was a map — like Captain Kidd made — on cloth, drawn with dye. The map became soaked and ruined. I want you to hear each boy's story," concluded Boyd.

Eddie, a youth of 20, told his story first.

"We lay becalmed at low tide off Brake Island," he said. "I was in the salon when I noticed a hole in the side no more than six inches above the waterline.

"I plugged the hole with a piece of folded cloth — I didn't realize it was the map! — I found under the desk. I don't know how it got there, I swear. When the tide rose, the map became wet."

Carl, the older brother, told a different story.

"Eddie was sore because I didn't immediately promise to share my treasure with him. I saw him sneak out of the salon and throw something overboard — a balled-up piece of cloth.

"Suspicious, I dived after it. The water was clear and calm as glass. I recovered the cloth immediately — but too late! On board, I saw it was the map, ruined!"

When Boyd was again alone with Haledjian, he said: "I can't verify Eddie's story about a hole near the waterline. I simply don't know who is lying!"

Haledjian knew. Do you?

Eddie lied. The sailboat would have risen with the tide, and so the water would never have reached the hole and wet the map.

The Case of the
Two Bank Robbers

Until Dr. Haledjian read the account, there never had been a question of the fate of the two men who robbed the bank at Silver City in '81.

Obviously, they had drowned in the Ki River.

The facts were:

The night before the robbery, Luke Tigert, the banker, brought his horse to Abe Wilson, the blacksmith. Abe was putting new shoes on two horses Luke had never seen before in Silver City, a huge piebald and a stubby bay mare.

Luke overheard Abe tell his helper the surprising fact that both horses wore the same size shoes.

The following afternoon, Abe and his helper robbed the bank. Abe rode off on the piebald, his helper on the little mare.

For several miles the pair kept to the mountains, whose rocky paths retained no hoofprints. Then, apparently confused in the gathering darkness, they cut across soft ground to the Ki River.

The two sets of hoofprints, one spaced farther apart than the other, were there for the posse to read in the morning.

The hoofprints led from the rocky path to a yard-wide gap in the bushes which ran along the river for several miles in each direction. A foot beyond the bushes, the ground dropped 200 feet to the water.

"The blacksmith's maneuver cleverly duped the posse," Haledjian told Octavia. "He let them think both riders and horses perished going over the cliff."

What had the blacksmith really done?

The blacksmith had ridden the huge piebald to the gap in the bushes. Then, to imitate the shorter stride of the little mare, he had returned the piebald to the rocky path — going backward.

A horse, like a man, takes shorter steps going backward than forward.

The Case of the
Two Mrs. Brauns

"Konrad Braun, the West German jeweler, died of natural causes last week in his hotel room," said Inspector Winters. "His estate, reputedly over half a million, will go to his bride."

"Bride?" Haledjian raised an eyebrow, "Braun was past seventy, wasn't he?"

"Apparently he married secretly just before sailing for America. He wired his American partner that his bride would join him in New York a week later. Other than that Mrs. Braun was a piano teacher, we don't know anything about her. Today she showed up — or two of them did. Both have all the necessary papers and know everything about Braun. But one is an imposter."

Haledjian consented to accompany the inspector to the home of the murdered man's American partner. In the living room, the two Mrs. Brauns, a blonde and a brunette, sat glowering at one another.

Both were robust, thirtyish, and pretty.

Haledjian shook hands first with the blonde, and winced. Her grip left a red welt where her ring had bitten into his fingers. The brunette, who looked equally formidable, wore rings on almost every finger. In self protection, Haledjian merely bowed. "Would you play the piano for me?" he requested.

The brunette went smoothly into a Chopin Nocturne, her muscular fingers a-glitter. Haledjian counted three sapphire rings and a wedding band on her left hand, and three diamonds of assorted sizes on her right.

When she finished, the blonde attacked the keyboard, playing the same nocturne as though to outshine her rival. Musically she did as well, though her single plain wedding band left her far behind in the jewelry contest.

When the last note died, Haledjian said, "Suppose you tell us why you are posing as Mrs. Braun!"

To which one did Haledjian speak?

To the bejeweled brunette, who wore her marriage ring on the left hand, the American custom. The blonde wore her band on the right hand (the hand she shook with) after the German tradition.

The Case of the
Unknown Blonde

"Pinky Kempton's story about a blonde in a plaid skirt and tight gray sweater is pretty weak," said Inspector Winters. "But unless we break it, we'll never find the gang who tried to hold up the National City Bank yesterday."

"You're convinced Kempton is involved?" asked Haledjian.

"He's been used as a lookout before," replied the inspector. "About the time of the holdup, two police officers noticed him loitering on the corner half a block from the bank.

"The way it figures is this," continued the inspector. "When things suddenly went wrong in the bank, the three masked bandits sprinted for their car. They didn't have time to haul in Kempton, so they left him on the corner.

"We picked him up this morning for questioning. He says he was out walking and had stopped to watch a blonde, whom nobody else on the block remembers seeing.

"This mysterious blonde, according to Kempton, was strolling on the opposite side of the street, looking over her left shoulder and primping herself in the reflection of the store windows.

"When she got to the Beford Shoe Store window, she stopped and slowly did an about-face. Watching her window image, she adjusted her skirt zipper and smoothed her sweater at the waist. She opened her purse, but noticing Kempton staring at her, hastened down the street.

"As she turned the corner, Kempton says three masked men dashed out of the bank and into a waiting sedan. He didn't get the license plate number, of course."

Haledjian pursed his lips thoughtfully. "Kempton's story has one slight flaw, inspector. Confront him with it, and he may break down."

What was the flaw?

According to Kempton, the blonde was looking over her left shoulder at her reflection, and then "did an about-face" and, still gazing at her reflection, "adjusted her skirt zipper." This meant she zipped her skirt on the right side. Unfortunately for Kempton, women's skirts zip on the left side.

The Case of the
Unknown Brother

Mrs. Sydney, New York's most illustrious party-giver, settled back in her dinner chair. With an eccentric smile, she applied herself to a favorite pastime — trying to confound the deductive prowess of Dr. Haledjian.

"My childhood playmate, Jedediah Wright, ran away from home when he was twelve," she began. "For years he lived by odd jobs. But in 1927 he settled in Michigan and made millions in copper.

"Unfortunately, Jed never married. On his deathbed he summoned his faithful housekeeper and handed her a fat envelope containing cash, deeds, and securities.

"His parents had passed away a decade earlier. Jed's only living kin was a brother. 'Give this envelope to my brother, Alf,' the dying man instructed the housekeeper.

"The poor, distracted woman had never seen Alf

in her life. Her only clue was a yellowed photograph set in a double frame with one of Jed. Unfortunately, the pictures were taken when both were boys of ten, fifty-five years before.

"Moreover, the only clue to Alf's whereabouts was a letter postmarked the previous month from Los Angeles.

"The housekeeper traveled to Los Angeles and advertised the purpose of her visit. Soon a hundred aged men were camped outside her hotel door.

"Although she had never seen Alf and knew nothing about him, she was able to pick him out of the bevy of imposters!"

"My dear Mrs. Sydney, to what ends will you go to stump an old sleuth?" said Haledjian with a reproachful sigh. "The answer is elementary."

How did the housekeeper know Alf?

Because of her one clue — and yours — the photograph. It was taken "when both boys were ten," fifty-five years ago." Hence, Alf and Jed were twins!

The Case of the
Vanishing Hostage

Mrs. Sydney, the dowager who owned more of Manhattan Island than anyone since the Indians, had satisfied every whim save one. She had never stumped Dr. Haledjian.

So the master sleuth knew the game of outwit-the-detective was on again when Mrs. Sydney set down her after-dinner cordial and regarded him with a triumphant eye.

"A desperate thief," she began, "broke into a Miami Beach motel at 2 A.M. and knocked out the night clerk. The clerk, however, recovered quickly and called the police.

"When they arrived, the detective in charge shouted to the thief to give himself up as the motel was surrounded.

"The thief was in suite 113, occupied by a Detroit family — a grandmother, a mother, and two daughters. He ordered the grandmother to the window and gave the terrified woman a message to relay through the window.

"The grandmother informed the detective that the thief would release three women on the condition that he withdraw his men for half an hour.

"Thinking quickly, the detective shouted back — "

Mrs. Sydney paused, smiling craftily. "Now, doctor, can you tell me what the detective shouted back that permitted all the women — the grandmother, mother, and two daughters — to walk out of the motel unharmed?"

"Really, madame," Haledjian reproached. "I should take offense at such an old word-teaser in new trimmings. The detective shouted — "

What?

The detective shouted back, "Agreed."
The grandmother, mother, and two daughters marched out unharmed, for they numbered only three persons.
The mother was both mother and daughter.

The Case of the
Water Nymph

Ivers, the insurance adjuster, passed the auction brochure to Dr. Haledjian and tapped a line.

Haledjian read, "Item 37, Water Nymph, undetermined alloy. Weight, 26 pounds. Height, 17½ inches."

"Thomas Covington purchased the statue three weeks ago at this auction in Los Angeles for $20," said Ivers. "He had it added to his personal property policy, placing the value at $10,000. It never arrived at his New York City apartment. He's put in a claim for $10,000!"

"What proof is there that it is lost?"

"The auction manager told me he mailed it to Covington's New York address," replied Ivers. "But, said the manager, he never was advised of its new worth, and so he sent it by ordinary mail — uninsured and unregistered. We can't trace it!"

"Can Covington substantiate its jump in value?"

"The jump is legitimate," replied Ivers. "A Texas oil man arrived too late to bid on the statue. He telephoned Covington at his Los Angeles hotel, explained the statue was a long-lost heirloom, and offered $10,000 for it.

"Covington agreed to sell the statue when he reached New York. He added it to his insurance but, he says, forgot to notify the auction house about the increased value."

"So your company will have to find the statue or pay the claim," said Haledjian.

The criminologist smiled and added:

"Covington and the auction manager are in cohoots. They plan to collect the insurance money and then sell the statue, getting $20,000 for a $20 investment!"

What made Haledjian so sure?

The auction manager's story of mailing the 26-pound statue to New York City was an obvious lie. The maximum weight the postal service will carry in first-class post offices, like New York City, is 25 pounds.

The Case of the
World Traveler

Moscow Memories, by Nina Virve, had been a runaway best-seller for three months when Dr. Haledjian received a telephone call from the book's publisher, Alf Shuller.

"When Mrs. Virve died last month, we held up the royalty payment," said Shuller. "She left no kin, or so we thought. But a husband who, according to the book, died in Odessa in 1910, has turned up, claiming the royalties. He'll be in my office at ten. Can you come over?"

Haledjian agreed, and in the publisher's office met Gregori Virve, a distinguished looking gentleman of seventy-odd, suitably equipped with a Russian passport, as well as with birth and marriage certificates.

After an exchange of pleasantries, Haledjian said, "Your wife wrote that you died of pneumonia. Curious you didn't inform her that you survived."

"Curious by American standards only," replied Virve. "You see, the marriage was arranged by our parents. It was short, unhappy. Six months after the wedding I contracted smallpox, not pneumonia. Through a mix-up at the hospital, my death was falsely recorded. I decided against correcting the error."

"My compliments on your English," said Haledjian. "I suppose you prospered and traveled a good bit since your alleged death."

"As Boris Novak I was quite successful in the textile line. Two years after my reported demise, I sold my business to a large Leningrad firm, retaining a share in the profits. Since then I've traveled extensively. When I collect the money from Nina's book, I intend to settle in London permanently. I have no love for my native land under the Communists."

After Virve departed, Alf Shuller said, "Everything appears in order. What do you think, doctor?"

"I'd let Inspector Winters examine his papers. I've a strong feeling they are forgeries."

Why did Haledjian believe the husband to be an imposter?

The report of Virve's death was issued in 1910, and yet the man claiming to be Virve said he'd sold his business two years later to a "large Leningrad firm" — a slip a real Russian, much less an outspoken anti-Communist, never would have made.

In 1912 Leningrad was still called St. Petersburg.

STILL MORE
TWO-MINUTE
MYSTERIES

For Kaethe Spiegel

The Case of the
Arctic Explorer

Sir James Harvey, aged bachelor and famed explorer of the North Pole, was found murdered in his bedroom.

The $400,000 in thousand-dollar bills, which he was known to keep in his wall safe, was missing.

The police concluded that the criminal or criminals had concealed the money in the house, perhaps in something brought along for the purpose, expecting to recover it later.

This surmise was founded upon Sir James's eccentric precautions. A visitor might gain admission to his estate unchallenged. But no one, including the servants, could leave without being challenged by a series of private guards.

On the day Sir James's possessions were put on auction, Dr. Haledjian joined Sheriff Monahan in the explorer's museum.

"The sale starts in here," said the sheriff. "But

every stick in the house will be sold today or to-morrow."

An auctioneer had begun to enumerate for the crowd of buyers the museum's objects, describing them as Sir James's favorite mementos of his five trips to the Arctic.

The objects included a group of stuffed animals — two polar bears and a penguin — three stuffed fish, and an assortment of Eskimo clothing, utensils, and weapons.

"The murderer has to be in the house," said the sheriff. "But my men can't watch all the rooms."

"Rest at ease," said Haledjian. "He or an accomplice is in this room, ready to make a purchase."

How did Haledjian know?

Haledjian realized the criminal had hidden the money in his own prop — the one thing in the museum which didn't belong with a collection of North Pole objects. The stuffed penguin.

The criminal forgot that penguins live in the South, not the North, Pole!

The Case of the
Arrowless Bow

The chief clue in the death of Bart Weaver was an archery bow, lying on the carpet at the top of a narrow twisting flight of stairs in his home.

"Weaver was found at the bottom of the stairs, his neck broken," Inspector Winters told Dr. Haledjian. "Had he fallen, his momentum would not have carried him around the twists in the stairs. He was pushed, and hard.

"As far as we can determine, the only thing missing from the house is Weaver's famous Luzon diamond. My theory is that Weaver heard burglars. Fearing for the diamond, he tied it to an arrow and shot it out this open window, expecting to reclaim it later."

"An exotic theory, but perhaps true," said Haledjian.

"Our prime suspect is Hugh Tiff. He's been trying to buy the diamond for years," said the inspector. "I'm having him picked up."

Haledjian hid the bow. The two men descended the stairs just as Tiff was brought in by two police-men.

Tiff listened arrogantly as the inspector said, "Bart Weaver was pushed down these stairs and killed. The Luzon diamond is missing. Were you in this house during the past three hours?"

"No, and I don't know a thing about Weaver's death," insisted Tiff. "But find the diamond, you dumb cop! I'll buy it!"

"The diamond won't be hard to locate," said Haledjian. And staring up at the top of the narrow staircase, he added, "It's only an arrow flight away."

"Then let's go outside and look!" exclaimed Tiff.

"Arrest him," snapped Haledjian.

How come?

As Haledjian stared at the stairs, Tiff, had he really known nothing, would have heard the sleuth say, ". . . a narrow flight away," not ". . . an arrow flight away."

Tiff should have said to look for the diamonds upstairs, not "outside."

The Case of the
Barbecue Murder

"Bill would have met your train himself, Dr. Haledjian," said Nora Perkins. "But since I was in town,
he asked me to pick you up. He wanted more time
to prepare the barbecue."

Bill Perkins, however, was past worrying about
barbecues when Haledjian and his hostess arrived
at the house half an hour later. Nora shrieked. Her
husband lay on the lawn, a knife protruding from
his chest.

A hasty examination indicated to Haledjian that
the killing had occurred about an hour before. He
studied the scene.

A half-cooked steak lay above flameless coals
banked in a stone barbecue pit. Upon an iron shelf
were a tray of condiments and a long-handled knife
and fork.

"Who are you?" demanded Haledjian as a young
man burst through the woods.

"Ed Magden. My house is about a hundred yards back there. I heard a shriek — what's happened?"

"Where were you an hour ago?" inquired Haledjian.

"Over at the boat yard. I'd just entered my driveway when I heard a shriek," replied Magden. "Here — what's this?"

Magden pointed to a metallic object partly buried under the coals. With a quick stride, he reached the pit, thrust in his hand, and pulled out a charred earring.

"Why, it's mine," gasped Nora. Suddenly her expression hardened. "Ed Magden, you hated Bill. What are you trying to do?"

"You hated him more than anyone," snapped back Magden.

"You hated enough to kill," Haledjian said to — *Which one?*

Ed Magden, who claimed to have just arrived. Yet he knew the coals were sufficiently cool for him to "thrust in" his hand among them.

Haledjian reasoned he had planted the earring to throw suspicion on Nora.

302

The Case of the
Bathing Beauty

"Bill Doyle killed Kitty Parker, all right," said Sheriff Monahan. "The only question is, was it premeditated, or did he kill in a moment of insanity?

"Whichever the jury decides will determine whether he lives or dies," the sheriff added as he and Dr. Haledjian took seats in the courtroom.

As the spectators crowded in, the sheriff gave Haledjian the details of the case.

"Kitty broke off with Doyle three weeks ago. He still carried a torch. But she dated freely.

"On the day of her death, she left work at two P.M. It was blazing hot, and she walked to the lake carrying her bathing suit wrapped in a towel. A lot of the young fellows noticed her. They had to — she was wearing a white blouse, tight gold toreador pants, and high-heeled gold sandals.

"There's an empty shack at the lake that's used as a place to change. Kitty got into her bikini and folded her clothes on the single bench.

"About three o'clock another girl reached the shack and discovered Doyle strangling Kitty. He insisted he was trying to revive her, and that he'd seen a tramp running away a moment before.

"At headquarters Doyle confessed to killing Kitty himself. 'She wouldn't come back to me,' he said. 'So I tried to scare her. I snatched her slip from among her clothes and wound it around her neck. She struggled . . . it was an accident!'

"Now," concluded the sheriff, "we'll see if the jury believes he only meant to scare her."

"They won't," said Haledjian.

Why not?

Obviously, Doyle had brought along a slip to use in strangling Kitty, believing, if caught, he might blame her murder on blind impulse.
But Kitty would never have worn a slip that day. Not underneath a pair of tight toreador pants.

The Case of the
Big Dipper

"Curtis Brown was shot to death between ten and eleven o'clock last night," Inspector Winters told Dr. Haledjian.

"The body was found at midnight in the kitchen of his home by his mother. She telephoned headquarters at once.

"Brown was a wealthy bachelor. His estate will be divided evenly between his mother and Tim Brown, a nephew. That automatically makes Tim suspect number one."

"Has he an alibi?" inquired Haledjian.

"He claims he never left the roof of his house from nine last night till four this morning," replied the inspector. "Tim's recently become a camera fiend. He says he spent the night photographing the stars."

The inspector handed Haledjian a folder thick with large photographs of the heavens.

"Tim says he was taking these pictures at the time

of the murder," the inspector went on. "His house is a two-hour drive from his uncle's."

The inspector tapped a photograph marked "one-hour exposure."

"He insists he took this picture between nine thirty and ten-thirty last night."

Haledjian studied the photograph — a beautifully clear shot of the Big Dipper.

The inspector said, "If Tim really clicked his lens on at nine-thirty and off at ten-thirty, he couldn't have traveled two hours and killed his uncle between ten and eleven."

"I'm not an astrologist," replied Haledjian. "But from reading the stars in this photograph, I predict a cloudy future for Mr. Tim Brown!"

Why?

Tim Brown could not have made a "beautifully clear shot" of the Big Dipper with his lens open an hour. The camera would have moved, due to the rotation of the earth, causing the stars on the photograph to appear as lines!

The Case of the
Birdwatcher

The body in the woods brought Dr. Haledjian's early morning nature walk to an abrupt end.

As he reached the summit of a little rise, he found Arthur Bently, well-known nature writer and a life-long birdwatcher, lying on the downward slope. Death was due to a high-powered rifle bullet that had entered at the base of the skull.

Ascertaining that the killing had occurred about an hour before, or around seven A.M., Haledjian retraced Bently's steps. The rains of the previous night had washed the dirt trail smooth, and Bently's fresh footprints were easy to follow.

The trail led due west with arrowlike straightness back to Bently's summer bungalow.

Bob Hilton, the dead man's secretary, collapsed into a fireside chair when he heard the news.

"What was Bently doing out in the woods by himself?" questioned Haledjian.

"He went off birdwatching," said Hilton. "He liked to go out alone."

"Did you hear a shot?"

"Yes, but this is hunting season. The sound of guns is quite common," replied Hilton. "It must have been an accident. Mr. Bently had no enemies."

"I'll have to call the police," said Haledjian. "And while they're getting here, you'd better think up a better story than the one you told me!"

How come?

Bently had been walking due east when he was shot. His direction gave the lie to Hilton's claim that he had gone off birdwatching.

An experienced birdwatcher like Bently would never walk due east, or into the rising sun, for he would perceive only the silhouettes of the birds against the bright sky!

The Case of the
Black Hat

Inspector Winters handed Dr. Haledjian a woman's crumpled black hat.

"In fashion lingo, it's called chic," said the inspector. "To me it's a clue — the only one — to the murderer of Marcia Davenport."

"The society beauty who was discovered early this morning near Route 22, strangled to death?" asked Haledjian.

"Yes. She was found wearing a sequinned black evening gown, satin pumps, a mink wrap, and black gloves — and she was bareheaded."

The inspector switched on his office intercom. "Bring in Ken Fowler."

Fowler, a handsome young man, glowered defiantly. Answering the inspector's question, he snapped, "Sure I left the party early last night — I hate those fancy shindigs. But I didn't take Marcia home in my car. I went alone."

"We have a witness," said the inspector. "Bill Betts, Marcia's escort. He insists she left early, with you. He found this hat in your car. I've already shown it to Betts, and he says he thinks it's the one she was wearing when she left. And her roommate says it was Marcia's hat, all right."

"Anybody could have stolen the hat and planted it in my car," growled Fowler.

"You were in love with Miss Davenport?"

"Yes — and so were half the men at the formal last night. Including your prize witness, Bill Betts."

Dismissing Fowler after a few more questions, the inspector asked Haledjian for his opinion.

"I think you can make an arrest," said the criminologist.

Arrest whom?

Bill Betts. Haledjian knew he'd planted the hat in his rival's car and concocted the story of Marcia Davenport having worn it to the formal.

Unfortunately for the jealous Betts, a woman doesn't wear a hat with an evening gown.

The Case of the
Bushwhackers

As the burro tossed and jolted, Haledjian wondered what madness had prompted him to sign up for this mountain ride. He should have remained at the resort on a beach chaise and let local color alone.

"That there's the Johnny Kid's corner," suddenly announced the tour's grizzly little guide. He pointed to a projection of rock which formed a perfect corner. "Seventy years ago on that spot, Ringo Charlie got bushwhacked by Johnny Kid. Johnny Kid objected to Ringo Charlie's weakness for palmin' aces. As Ringo Charlie was the fastest gun in three counties and related to half the town, Johnny Kid never pushed his objections. But one fine day he crouched behind that there rock and waited."

The guide dismounted and briefly made like Johnny Kid.

"'Long about four in the afternoon," he resumed, "Ringo Charlie and his brother Sy come along. They'd suspicion'd somethin'. So they'd left the horses back a piece and come up quiet, on foot."

The guide rose from his knee, rounded the corner, and walked a dozen paces. He turned about, enacting the part of Ringo Charlie, and sneaked toward the corner. He squinted dramatically into the afternoon sun and held one hand cupped above the butt of an imaginary pistol.

"Johnny Kid seen Ringo Charlie's shadow comin' while Ringo was still six feet away. Out jumps the Kid, two guns blazin'. Ringo Charlie goes flat as a slab, and Sy hightails it back to town for a posse.

"A fair fight was one thing, but bushwhackin' was another breed of cow. When folks heerd how Johnny Kid had the advantage on Ringo Charlie, they up and lynched him, even though the Kid don't yet have any chin fuzz."

"They hanged an innocent boy," said Haledjian.

The guide stared. "W-what's that?"

"Sy lied to the townsfolk. I suppose he hated to admit a mere boy beat his brother to the draw," said Haledjian.

What was amiss with the story Sy told the towns-folk?

Sy said Johnny Kid knew his brother was coming because at four o'clock his shadow, falling ahead of him, gave him away, yet the guide, in retracing Ringo Charlie's approach, had "squinted . . . into the afternoon sun."

With the sun in his face, Ringo Charlie's shadow would have fallen *behind* him.

The Case of the
Body by the Garage

The bulb hung directly above the upturned hood of a white sports car. Through the open garage doors the dim yellow light reached into the night and illuminated the body of a man dressed in oil-splotched loafers, greasy wool shirt, and dirty blue jeans.

He might have been slumbering, except that his head was savagely crushed in.

"Roger Pratt, the socialite playboy," said Inspector Winters. "Mrs. Pratt's nurse saw the whole thing. It was she who summoned the police."

Inside the house, Bertha Tone, the nurse, repeated her story for Dr. Haledjian.

"I was with Mrs. Pratt all night. Mr. Pratt said she was not to be left alone. She's been very ill.

"About midnight I glanced through the bedroom window and saw Mr. Pratt step out of the garage. A woman slipped from behind those bushes and struck him over the head with some instrument."

313

"Didn't Mr. Pratt notice his assailant's approach?"

"It all happened too swiftly. As Mr. Pratt stooped to tie his shoelaces, the woman darted up behind him. I don't think he saw or heard her. I immediately called the police from the telephone in the bedroom."

"You didn't leave the house tonight?"

"No," replied the nurse, stiffening.

The nurse's statement was confirmed by Mrs. Pratt. "Bertha made a telephone call about midnight. Whispered so I couldn't hear! A little later she answered the doorbell. Otherwise she didn't leave me. What's the girl been up to?"

"She went downstairs to open the door for Inspector Winters and me," said Haledjian. "And she's been up to murder!"

What was wrong with the nurse's story?

In asserting the dead man stooped over to tie his shoelaces, Berta Tone lied damningly. Roger Pratt was wearing loafers.

She had no reason to lie unless involved in the crime.

314

The Case of the
Bogus Hero

"Last night I had my lines down pat — yet something went wrong," moaned Cyril Makin, the would-be ladykiller. "Marjorie saw right through me."

He sighed. "Marjorie is Marjorie Appelson. She's the daughter of old General William 'Wild Bill' Appelson and she's positively flip over war heroes. I was a veterinary's aide in Korea and never heard a gun go off. So I had to invent a gutsy, front-line story to score with her."

"Perhaps if you tell me exactly what you told her, I might detect your mistake," suggested Haledjian.

The youth looked embarrassed, but he repeated his trumped-up tale for Haledjian.

"I was in an advanced post with some mortarmen when suddenly I heard rustling in the woods to our left. As it was a hot, windless day, I guessed what caused the rustling — the enemy.

"Presently they charged us. But I'd alerted our

315

boys, and we countered with everything we had. They retreated, leaving a hundred dead.

"I'd just picked up a pair of field glasses from a dead captain when somebody shouted, 'More coming!'

"A column of infantry was approaching. We were all set to hit 'em with mortars when I cried, 'Hold your fire! They're Americans!'

"Later, I explained to the colonel that I'd spotted his regimental flag flying. He shook my hand and declared but for my quick thinking, his whole regiment would have been wiped out by our mortars!"

As Cyril finished, Haledjian chuckled. "I don't wonder Miss Appelson didn't believe you."

Why not?

As it was a "hot, windless day," the regimental flag could not have been "flying." Obviously, Cyril could not have identified a regimental flag, or any other flag, hanging limp.

The Case of the
Bomb Thrower

Lying in the tree house, young Jimmy Metz looked across the street and saw the lights go off in the house belonging to Brett Hall, the outspoken candidate for the state senate.

Jimmy checked his watch. Ten past midnight.

Deciding that a tree house wasn't such a hot place to spend the night after all, Jimmy was about to start for bed. Then he noticed the convertible.

It was creeping slowly along the deserted streets, its lights out. As it passed under the street lamp, Jimmy saw a man behind the wheel, another standing in the back.

"Aim for the bay window," said the driver. "And don't throw a fifty-eight-footer."

"Don't worry," said the standing man.

He drew back his arm and threw. Then the car shot away in a roar of acceleration.

A moment later the bomb exploded on Brett Hall's lawn.

Inspector Winters, investigating the case, questioned young Jimmy at great length. But the boy could provide no further information.

"Hall has received several threatening letters during the campaign," the inspector told Dr. Haledjian later. "The bomb apparently was intended to explode inside the house, but the bomber misjudged the distance. I doubt if we'll ever catch him."

"You've got one excellent lead," said Haledjian. "I should concentrate on the local baseball teams. Start your questioning with the catchers."

How come?

Everyone knows it's sixty feet, six inches from the pitching rubber to home plate, but only catchers call those low pitches which bounce in front of the plate "fifty-eight-footers."

The Case of the
Civil War Saber

"From the length of your face I deduce it was slapped by some young lady whose good opinion you were endeavoring to win, but which you lost instead," said Dr. Haledjian.

"Quite right, as usual," muttered Cyril Makin, the capsizing Casanova. "This time I even went out and got a prop — a saber — to lend my story authenticity.

"You've heard of General R. Horatio Abercrombie? The old walrus fought for the Union during the Civil War. His great-great-granddaughter, Matilda, is secretary of the Civil War Round Table. She won't give you a tumble unless your great-great-grandfather fought in the great American conflict too.

"Unfortunately," went on Cyril, "both my great-great-grandparents were London chimney sweeps. They never fought anything but soot. So to impress Matilda, I invented an ancestor, Lieutenant George

Makin, 79th New York Highlanders.

"I told Matilda that at the first battle of Bull Run, when the commanding officer was killed, Lieutenant Makin took over the regiment and saved it from annihilation. Again, at the second battle of Bull Run, the year following, he rallied the troops despite the loss of one hundred and five men.

"The month after First Bull Run, the men of his company presented George with a saber. Here I showed Matilda the saber I'd purchased at a costumer's shop and had inscribed:

"To Lt. G. Makin, for gallantry at First Bull Run, July 21, 1861, from the men of his company, in appreciation.

"I was feeling pretty cocky when I gave her the blade — "

"And then she promptly gave you the gate," said Haledjian. "I hardly blame her!"

What was Cyril's mistake?

As the second battle of Bull Run did not occur until "the year following," the first, the men of Lt. Makin's company could not have known "the month after First Bull" that there would be a second battle. They would have inscribed the blade ". . . at Bull Run," and not ". . . at First Bull Run."

The Case of the
Dead Man's Medals

The death of John Marks III of heart failure deprived the world of one of its leading philanthropists.

Marks, the only child of a former governor, and a bachelor, had devoted most of his life to the welfare of underprivileged children throughout the world.

Dr. Haledjian was among the many mourners who visited the Marks home on the hottest day of the year.

After viewing the body in the bedroom, the famed sleuth passed through the sweltering, crowded living room and into the library.

Here were displayed the awards given the deceased by many heads of state for his work with children. Some of the medals, inlaid with jewels, were worth thousands of dollars.

Haledjian had just nodded at the uniformed guard in the room when somebody shouted for a doctor.

Haledjian and the guard hurried into the living

room, which had been thrown into a great commotion.

A young man wearing a dark gabardine suit was carrying a young lady in his arms toward the front door.

When the photographer from the local paper hurried up, the young man at first looked flustered. Then he snapped: "Please, no pictures. This is the deceased's niece, Vivian Farns. Show some respect. Let me get her outside."

Quickly Haledjian directed the guard to detain the pair.

Then he raced back into the library in time to prevent a thief from making off with the valuable collection of medals.

What made Haledjian suspicious?

The girl's fainting spell was obviously a decoy to lure the guard from the library.

She could not have been the niece of the deceased man, who had been a bachelor and an only child.

The Case of the
Dead Recluse

The body of Mrs. Frieda Beck, eighty-nine years old, was discovered in the kitchen of her three-room apartment where she had lived as a recluse for fifty years.

Police found one of the gas jets of her four-jet range on. Death was established as due to gas poisoning from the jet.

According to neighborhood gossip, the elderly woman had a fortune in cash hidden in the apartment.

"It looked at first like murder in the course of attempted robbery," Inspector Winters told Dr. Haledjian. "But Mrs. Beck's pocketbook, containing $219, was untouched on a love seat in the next room. An intruder would have spotted it right away.

"The janitor says a bill collector had asked him to investigate after finding the apartment door locked. The janitor says he refused, because Mrs. Beck had left strict orders never to be disturbed. He did nothing for an hour. Then, realizing he hadn't seen Mrs. Beck for longer than usual, he grew worried. Accompanied by the beat policeman, he unlocked the door. She was already dead."

"Was the apartment ransacked?" asked Haledjian.

"It was neat as a pin. But the window to the fire escape in the living room was unlocked," replied the inspector. "Since the janitor is the only person with a key beside the victim, we're holding him on suspicion. He insists he's innocent."

"I'm sure he is," said Haledjian. "Death was accidental. Only a master murderer could have staged such a scene."

What did Haledjian mean?

jets — and left them on — to make sure of the job.
The amateur killer would have turned on all four
dental.
and turned off three jets to make death look acci-
died things up, ignored the cash in the pocketbook,
apartment for the rumored fortune, would have ti-
Only an experienced killer, after searching the

The Case of the
Death by the Tracks

The fat man lay by the railroad embankment, his horribly twisted limbs testifying to the imprudence of leaving a train as it raced at a hundred miles per hour.

"Broken neck — probably killed on impact," said Dr. Haledjian after a summary examination. "Who is he?"

"Tommy Warner, the New York racketeer," replied Sheriff Monahan. "He must have jumped from the Rocket. It leaves Chicago for Los Angeles on Tuesday night and passes through here around four Wednesday afternoon. It's the only train by today."

"What makes you sure Warner jumped?" asked Haledjian.

"For one thing, the money in his wallet. For another, his valises."

"Valises?"

"I'll show you," said the sheriff, shading his eyes

as he led the way down the tracks toward the setting sun.

After some five hundred yards, the two men came to the first valise. It contained expensive clothes, monogrammed TW.

Two hundred yards further along lay the second valise. It contained $50,000 in new twenty-dollar bills.

"Counterfeit," said the sheriff. "Apparently someone wanted it, and Warner decided to jump rather than give it up."

"At least that's what someone wants the authorities to believe," said Haledjian. "The killer went to a lot of trouble, but Warner was thrown from the train."

How did Haledjian know?

The two valises were found far to the west of the body ("toward the setting sun"), in the same direction as the train traveled (Chicago to Los Angeles). Hence, Warner had left the speeding train first and his bags had followed him several seconds later.

The Case of the
Death in the Air

The ancient tri-prop airplane had barely taken off from Nigeria when it encountered violent turbulence. After half an hour in the air, Dr. Haledjian's hopes of completing the bumpy trip in undisturbed misery were shattered by the steward.

"Come quickly, Dr. Haledjian!"

Musing on the inconveniences of fame, Haledjian groped along the storm-tossed cabin. In the front seat, a man sat lifeless, a knife in his heart.

Near the death seat was a small desk. On it lay a pad of legal-size sheets filled out in perfect handwriting.

"I was doing my manifests," said the steward. "Five minutes ago I heard a grunt, but thought nothing of it. A moment ago, I turned around and found passenger Alo like that."

Haledjian walked back up the aisle. The nine-seat

plane held only three other passengers. All appeared to be dozing.

In the middle of the plane a fat man sat in stocking feet. One shoe lay on the seat beside him, the other on the floor.

The last two seats were occupied by a young couple. The man held the girl by the left wrist. She sat rigidly, teeth bared, as if suffering from fright.

Haledjian advised the pilot to alert the police, and when the plane landed, he told the officer in charge: "Arrest — "

Whom?

The steward. He could not have filled out the manifest with "perfect handwriting" during the storm-tossed flight.

The Case of the
Doubting Uncle

"Are you sure no one has entered this room since your uncle's suicide?" asked Dr. Haledjian.

"Positive," replied young Lloyd Carstairs. "I have the only key."

It had been four days since Henry Fitzsimmons had taken his own life. He had left notes for the two men who now prepared to enter his bedroom.

In the notes, Fitzsimmons requested that a four-day waiting period be observed before the room was entered and the safe behind his portrait opened.

The $100,000 therein was to be divided equally between his alma mater and his only kin, young Carstairs.

Haledjian walked to the fireplace, above which hung the portrait of the deceased. A plant was set on the mantel, its broad leaves turned to the wall and touching the canvas.

Haledjian carefully removed the plant, lest he

329

knock it over, and swung back the portrait.

"Suppose you open the safe," he said to Carstairs. "I believe your note included the combination too."

While the youth worked the dial, Haledjian crossed to the sunny window directly opposite the portrait. The window was locked from the inside.

There was a click. The youth cried, "The safe's empty!"

"Of course," said Haledjian. "I have the money, which your uncle sent me. He wanted to test you — to see if you'd try to open the safe before the four days elapsed."

"I never was in here!" insisted the youth.

"A bad lie," said Haledjian. "And a costly one. Now all the money will go to your uncle's alma mater."

What was the youth's mistake?

The window was locked from the inside, and the youth had the only key. Hence it had to be he who, in secretly opening the safe, replaced the plant so that the leaves were "turned to the wall."

Untouched in four days, the leaves should have been turned toward the window and the sun.

The Case of the
Dowager's Jewels

Mrs. Sydney, the dowager who was reputed to own eight and a quarter percent of New York City, had gratified every whim but one.

She had never confounded the master sleuth, Dr. Haledjian.

So Haledjian was on his guard when, after a sip of Vichy water, Mrs. Sydney leaned back in her dinner chair and related her most recent harrowing experience.

"You shall hardly believe how close I came to losing my life and jewels last night," she began.

"It must have been around three A.M. when a noise awoke me. A masked man was standing in my room, pointing a gun at me and ordering me not to cry out.

"By the moonlight, I could see two more men climbing through the open window. I was bound and gagged and brutally thrown on my back on the bed while the horrible creatures went through my jewels.

"Helpless, I watched the fiends fill a sack with gems. For fear of my life, I did not dare do anything till they had started out the window.

"As the last of them went out, I screamed for help. Fortunately, Patrolman Casey was a block away and heard me. The thieves dropped the jewels in their haste to escape from him, but I shall be a month recovering from the fright!"

Haledjian smiled appreciatively.

"My dear Mrs. Sydney," he said. "Your convalescence from an experience that never happened will undoubtedly be short."

What was wrong with her story?

As Mrs. Sydney was "helpless," having been bound and "gagged," it would have been impossible for her to cry out loud enough for Patrolman Casey, "a block away," to have heard her.

The Case of the
Dropped Cuff Link

"My latest case," said Sheriff Monahan to Dr. Haledjian "required some rapid deduction that would have done you credit."

The sheriff leaned back in his chair, took a long drag on his cigar, and with an air of contentment recounted the details.

"A single gunman held up Brigs and Company and escaped with the entire monthly payroll. I got a tip that he would be aboard a train headed for Columbia, South Carolina, that afternoon.

"I caught the train. Unfortunately, I didn't know what my man looked like. I could only keep watch for anyone acting suspiciously.

"The conductors helped me. They reported that the occupant of lower nine in car eleven fifty-five was the only passenger who kept his face hidden. He had poked his ticket through the curtain of his berth.

"To get a look at him, I took the berth above his, and purposefully dropped a cuff link down on him. There was no place for him to hide — not with me suddenly hanging head down next to him.

"Alas, he was reading a newspaper, held full length before him. I told him about the cuff link, and he told me to 'beat it,' without showing his face.

"I thought I'd flubbed till I caught a glance at the headlines of his paper: LONE BANDIT ESCAPES WITH 100G PAYROLL."

"You arrested him, I presume?" asked Haledjian.

"On the spot," replied the sheriff.

What gave the holdup man away?

The fact that the sheriff, hanging head down, could read the headlines at a glance meant that the newspaper was turned the same way. Hence the man in lower nine was "reading" it upside down!

The Case of the
Edmund Bayne

Dr. Haledjian was driving past the small home of Edmund Bayne, a retired army officer, when he saw a young man dash out of the front door.

"Help!" he shouted. "Somebody get a doctor!"

Haledjian offered his services, and the youth hurried him into the house.

Beside the telephone table in the foyer lay the body of Edmund Bayne.

"Who is he?" exclaimed the young man. "Are you a friend?"

"Yes — he was Ed Bayne. Don't you know him?"

The youth shook his head. "Never heard of him."

"Ed's been retired for fifteen years," said Haledjian. "I didn't think he had an enemy in the world. How did you happen to find him?"

"I was running for the bus when I heard a shot from this house. I found the front door unlocked and him lying like that."

335

Haledjian's swift examination disclosed that death, from a bullet wound in the heart, had occurred within the past few minutes. A French Army pistol lay beside the body.

"Call the police," advised Haledjian. "The number is 666-4551."

The youth dialed and spoke excitedly.

"Hello, police? Somebody shot Edmund Bayne! Where? Oh, on High Street . . . middle of the block . . . brick house . . . ah . . ."

"The address is 621 High Street," said Haledjian. "As if you don't know!"

Why did he doubt the youth?

The youth claimed he had "never heard" of Edmund Bayne. Yet he told the police the dead man's name was Edmund.

As Haledjian had told him only "Ed.," he could not have known whether it was Edmund, Edward, Edwin, or Edgar!

The Case of the
Fatal Oversight

It took only five minutes on a hot August night for Johnson to kill Kuto and rob him of $3,000.

Six minutes before eleven P.M., the time the main feature at the corner movie theater began, Johnson stepped across the hall and knocked at Kuto's door.

Being admitted, Johnson closed the door behind him. Kuto stared questioningly at Johnson's black-gloved hands; his eyes opened wide as Johnson drew his gun. The silencer whistled twice. Kuto fell.

Taking the dead man's keys, Johnson opened Kuto's strongbox and put $3,000 in cash into his pocket. Then he dialed the police.

"My name is Johnson," he said. "I'm calling from Mr. Kuto's apartment at 591 Grand Street. There's been a murder!"

Hanging up, Johnson slipped out of Kuto's apartment, dropped the gun down the garbage chute, and went across the hall to his own room. There he removed his gloves and hid the money.

He was waiting in Kuto's room when Inspector Winters arrived. He said: "It was too hot to sleep, so I decided to go to a movie. As I stepped into the hall, a big man dashed out of Kuto's door, knocked me down, tossed something into the garbage chute, and raced downstairs."

That night the inspector related the case to Dr. Haledjian, concluding with: "Johnson claimed he had not been in Kuto's apartment for a week. But after our lab boys got through there, Johnson confessed. I suppose you can guess why."

Haledjian guessed. Can you?

Although Johnson telephoned from Kuto's apartment, his fingerprints were not on the telephone.

He did not remove his gloves till after entering his own apartment — a fatal oversight on a hot August night!

338

The Case of the
Five Candidates

"Charles was going to announce his successor as president of Consolidated Coal and Oil at our home tonight," Mrs. Charles Twayne, widow of the murdered man, told Haledjian.

"Each of the five young men invited to dinner was a candidate," she continued. "However, as Charles left for the golf club this morning, he said he might eliminate one."

"At lunch time," interrupted Sheriff Monahan, "Mr. Twayne and Rick Donovan had an argument in the men's grille. Was Donovan the one eliminated, Mrs. Twayne?"

"I don't know," she replied. "Charles didn't say which one. When he came to the tenth tee, he saw me standing on the terrace and held up four fingers. 'Four!' he called to me, meaning I should set the table for four guests instead of five. A moment later he clutched his chest and toppled over."

"The killer used a silencer," said the sheriff. "I took a statement from Rick Donovan two hours after the shooting. He claims he left the club without knowing of Mr. Twayne's death."

Haledjian picked up Donovan's statement, written in the suspect's own hand. He glanced through it till he came to:

"I was playing the eighteenth and had hooked my drive into the bushes behind the tenth tee. As I searched for the ball, I heard Twayne shout, 'Four!' But I didn't see him because of the bushes. And, as I returned to my home without changing clothes, I knew nothing of his death for two hours."

"Donovan is lying," declared Haledjian. "Undoubtedly he was the one eliminated by Mr. Twayne for the presidency and took revenge by murder."

What tripped Donovan?

Donovan asserted he did not see Twayne on the tee, yet he knew Twayne shouted, "Four!"

Obviously, he'd seen Twayne signal his wife, or he would have written that Twayne shouted the golfer's warning, "Fore!"

The Case of the
Football Players

Dr. Haledjian and Sheriff Monahan sloshed ankle-deep in the chilly waters of huge lake Tomanachi as they walked by the outside of the nine-foot wall set in the sandy shallows behind the murdered woman's house.

"The wall completely encloses the house," said the sheriff. "Two hours ago, John Bookman came home from a late movie. He thought he saw a man going over the wall here."

The sheriff pointed to a homemade ladder leaning against the outside of the wall.

"It was pitch dark, and so Bookman decided he was imagining things — you'll notice the top of the ladder is four inches below the top of the wall, and so it can't be seen from the house side. Then he discovered his wife in the kitchen, stabbed to death.

"Bookman suspects her ex-boyfriend, Gary Mills, a professional football tackle, who has a cottage

341

across the lake. Mills, who owns a rowboat, insists he was home all night, but he has no corroborating witness."

Haledjian climbed the ladder, looked at the back of the Bookman house, and climbed down. The top of the ladder was now six inches below the top of the wall.

"Shall I arrest Mills?" asked the sheriff.

"No, Bookman," snorted Haledjian.

How come?

The ladder was an obvious prop to mislead the police.

No one — certainly not a ponderous professional tackle like Gary Mills — could have used it, since Haledjian's weight on it, after it supposedly had been used, caused the ladder to sink two inches more — from "four inches below the top of the wall" to "six inches."

342

The Case of the
Four-Footed Sleuth

"I suppose the Brandywine case is the only murder ever solved with the help of a chipmunk," said Dr. Haledjian.

"Sounds fascinating. Tell me about it!" begged Octavia.

"A highway patrolman," began the criminologist, "was driving in a sudden thunderstorm on Lakeview Drive when he spied an old, green convertible, top down, parked on a dirt side road.

"The fact that the convertible was empty, yet the horn was honking in wild spurts, caused the officer to investigate.

"The mystery seemed closed when he discovered a chipmunk had caught its hind leg in the horn mechanism. The officer freed the poor creature and as a matter of course noted down the car's license number.

"Two weeks later the body of Sylvia Brandywine

343

was found on the other side of the hill from the spot at which the convertible had been parked. Death, due to strangulation, had occurred about the day the convertible was sighted.

"The police backchecked and questioned the car's owner, Oscar Hayes, a pipe fitter. He admitted being out by the lake. However, he said he'd left the convertible when he couldn't start it. He denied leaving the car to hide the body.

"Phil Burger, manager of Ace Garage, said Hayes telephoned him to get the car. Burger found the battery absolutely dead and towed the car back to town.

"Burger and the police agreed Hayes was making his call about the time the convertible was found by the patrolman.

"Now," concluded Haledjian. "I was quite sure Hayes was lying — that he probably was off hiding the body of Miss Brandywine when the patrolman spied the car."

What was the giveaway?

Hayes needed an alibi for leaving his car with the top down in the rain. He lied in saying he couldn't start it since the battery could not have been "absolutely dead" or the chipmunk could not have made the horn honk. Burger was an accomplice.

344

The Case of the
Frightened Playboy

Answering an urgent telephone summons from the playboy, Jeff Lawry, Dr. Haledjian arrived at Lawry's penthouse a minute before seven A.M.

A tall woman was waiting at the penthouse door.

In a moment Haledjian and the tall woman were admitted by Lawry, who was clad in a bathrobe and green pajamas. He greeted Dr. Haledjian and stared suspiciously at the woman.

"I'm Clara Miley," she said. "The agency sent me."

"The new maid," exclaimed Lawry, obviously relieved. "Your room is that one. The kitchen is in the rear. I was about to have something to eat. Do you mind fixing me something?"

The woman strode off obediently. Lawry led Haledjian into the study and carefully closed the door.

"I've lived in absolute terror," confided the playboy, "since I saw those men rob the bank last week.

345

Do you know what I've been doing? Sleeping days and sneaking out nights!"

"Suppose we talk with Inspector Winters at headquarters," suggested Haledjian. "He'll give you protection."

"Not this morning," said Lawry wearily. "I've been awake all night. I'm going to bed."

Just then Clara Miley entered the study with a tray.

"I've fixed you a snack, sir," she said.

"That looks just fine," said Lawry, glancing at the glass of milk, ham sandwich, and layer cake. He picked up the milk.

"Don't drink it!" shouted Haledjian, seizing the new maid.

What alarmed Haledjian?

Only someone aware of Lawry's recent night habits would have prepared a "snack" of milk, sandwich, and cake at seven A.M.

Had Clara Miley really been just a maid, she would have fixed him breakfast; i.e., coffee, juice, eggs, etc.

The Case of the
Frozen Suspect

When the bitter cold that had frozen most of the Tahoo River practically all winter began to pass, a small boy noticed something red just below the surface.

It turned out to be a scarf — wrapped around the neck of a man. The body was further clothed in thick-soled shoes, two sweaters, rough trousers, work gloves, and a brown stocking cap.

Bud Kobs, missing since the previous November, had come to shore encased in a tomb of ice.

Kobs had been wanted in the slaying of Otis Ware. Art Byrnes, a partner with Ware and Kobs in a junkyard by the river, had witnessed the killing.

On the morning of November 23, while the men were moving a pile of pipes, Kobs and Ware fell to arguing, Byrnes had told the coroner's jury.

In a fit of rage, Byrnes said, Kobs had seized a three-foot length of cast iron pipe and hit Ware on

347

the head. Tossing the pipe away, Kobs had dashed for the frozen river.

He got halfway across, Byrnes said, and fell through the ice.

"Kobs couldn't swim," Sheriff Monahan told Dr. Haledjian the day after the body was found. "He must have banged his head on the ice and never regained consciousness. The autopsy showed a severe contusion on the base of the skull.

"Kobs had a criminal record," concluded the sheriff. "We matched his fingerprints against those on the pipe last November. He's the murderer, all right. Case closed!"

"Case nearly closed," corrected Haledjian.

Why not closed?

Haledjian deduced that Byrnes had slain both partners after contriving to get Kob's fingerprints on the pipe.

His story of an argument was patently false, since when Kobs was found he was wearing "work gloves," and hence could not have left fingerprints on the pipe during a fight.

The Case of the
Gas Station Murder

All the money — $14.19 — that Cal Peak had in his pockets when he was gunned down was spread on Sheriff Monahan's desk.

Dr. Haledjian fingered a two-dollar bill, one of four such. The rest of the money consisted of a five-dollar bill, a half-dollar, a quarter, four dimes, and four pennies.

"Odd that Peak should be carrying four two-dollar bills," said the famous sleuth. "Was there a reason?"

"No," replied the sheriff. "At least none that I can find. And there doesn't seem to be a reason for his killing.

"There was one witness," continued the sheriff. "Archie Kemp. Peak was sitting in Archie's gas station yesterday when, around noon, a man entered and asked for change. Archie didn't catch the sum, because just then he yawned. But Peak took out his money and said he could make change.

"Now here's the queer part," said the sheriff. "Archie heard the stranger say that he'd left his money in his car. So Peak followed him outside. Archie saw the stranger walk to a big yellow convertible. There was another man behind the wheel; he pulled a gun and shot Peak twice in cold blood. Then the convertible roared off. Archie was so dumbfounded he didn't even get the license number."

"For a good reason," said Haledjian. "Archie's account is a complete lie."

How did Haledjian know?

Archie said that Peak "took out his money and said he could make change" for the stranger. Impossible. He couldn't have made change for any bill or coin with the $14.19 found on his corpse.

The Case of the
Gasping Partner

Dr. Haledjian glanced at his watch — ten minutes to midnight — as he answered the telephone.

"Hello? This is Ben Bird!"came the excited voice. "I was just speaking to Clyde Linz on the telephone when I heard him gasp — then nothing. Something's happened! Can you meet me at his apartment right away?"

"I can be there in fifteen minutes," said the sleuth.

Bird and Linz, partners in a roofing business, lived in the fine old section of the city. Bird was waiting on the sidewalk when Haledjian arrived in a taxi.

They rode the elevator to Linz's floor. "I've got a key," said Bird, unlocking the door to Linz's small bachelor abode.

Linz was dead on the couch. A knife protruded from his chest.

Death had occurred within the hour, Haledjian found.

"Clyde telephoned me as I was going to bed," said Bird. "He said something urgent had come up. He wanted to speak with me right away. Suddenly he gave a hideous gasp. I dialed you immediately."

Haledjian noted the open window leading to the fire escape.

The telephone receiver hung off the cradle near the dead man's right hand.

"I'll notify the police," said Haledjian. "But before I do, you'd better stop lying!"

Why did he doubt Bird? (Look out. A toughie.)

Linz and Bird lived in the "fine old section of the city." Bird claimed that Linz telephoned him. But Bird also claimed that he telephoned Haledjian "immediately" afterward. Impossible! In the old sections of the city (pre-1957) only the person originating a telephone call could terminate it.

Linz's telephone was still off the hook. Therefore, Bird must have been holding a dead line!

The Case of the
Gold Brick

"My great-grandfather, Everet Lamont Sydney, panned gold from a secret stream and by 1875 was the richest man in California," said Mrs. Sydney, a sly twinkle in her eye.

"On his death bed, he told two old prospectors, Jepp Hanson and Oscar Tyre, the way to the stream and agreed to let them pan for gold, provided they swore never to divulge the location or make more than one trip themselves.

"Jepp and Oscar signed a contract, which stated: 'Whatever gold Jepp Hanson and Oscar Tyre or any individual in their expedition can carry by himself from the stream to the home of Everet Sydney shall be given said individual.'

"Naturally, Jepp and Oscar didn't bring anyone else in on their bonanza. They set out by themselves the next morning, having loaded Jepp's old mule with enough tools and provisions to stay in the wilds six months. They had hardly got to the stream when a landslide buried their equipment. All the two prospectors salvaged were the shorts they wore at night, the mule, and two pans.

"Since the contract said they could make only one trip, they stayed on, living off wild berries and nuts. After five months they got enough gold dust, which, to prevent from being blown away, they ingeniously melted into a brick. That small brick, measuring but a foot long, six inches wide, and six inches high, would make them millionaires.

"My great-grandfather died while they were away, and the two oldtimers took their case to court. Each insisted he had been the one who carried the brick.

"The judge peered at the brick and at the contract, and awarded the gold — to whom?"

Dr. Haledjian shook his head reproachfully. "My dear Mrs. Sydney. You are forever trying to trip up an old sleuth."

And so that the other guests couldn't hear, he whispered, "To — "

To whom?

The mule. Neither oldtimer could have carried the brick more than ten yards. A brick of gold, measuring one foot long by six inches wide by six inches high weighs over three hundred pounds.

The Case of the
Happy Baby

"John Wilson doesn't look much like a murderer," said Sheriff Monahan as a young man emerged from the farmhouse carrying a naked baby boy.

The sheriff stopped the patrol car behind Wilson's yellow sedan. He drew his pistol, whispered to Dr. Haledjian to wait, and called: "Raise your hands, John!"

Wilson halted, amazed. He sat his infant son carefully on the fender of his car and lifted his hands. "What's it all about, Sheriff?"

"Murder. We have a witness who says you entered Moose Long's bar last night after closing. Half an hour later Mrs. Long found Moose strangled to death with a yellow scarf."

"That's a lie. Why — "

"Look out!" cried Haledjian, as the baby scampered onto the yellow hood. Cooing happily, he attempted to stand. Haledjian just saved him from toppling to the ground.

"That witness is mistaken, Sheriff," Wilson resumed calmly. "I've been in this car since eight o'clock last night driving down from Philadelphia. I just arrived five minutes ago."

The sheriff looked at his watch. "Then you drove the six hundred miles between Philly and here in a little over twelve hours," he said dubiously.

"Can you prove I didn't?" snapped Wilson.

"Nothing could be easier," declared Haledjian. *What was wrong with Wilson's alibi?*

If Wilson had really arrived home "five minutes ago," having driven six hundred miles, the motor — and the hood — of his car would still be sizzling hot. The baby would have been screaming, not "cooing happily," standing on the hood.

The Case of the
Hidden Money

"Doc Everette is down with the flu," said Sheriff Kimball. "I hated to call you on such a hot day, but I need someone to sign the death certificate."

"Any reason to support foul play?" inquired Dr. Haledjian, kneeling beside the body of the wizened old recluse.

"None whatever. Old Carl lived up here alone with his cats. Sort of a character, you know, but harmless. He used to drive to town in a flivver once a week. Since he got the deep freeze installed last year, he came in every other month."

"When was his last trip?"

"Oh, maybe seven — eight weeks ago."

"I suppose the old man disliked banks as well as people?"

"There was that story. Life savings hidden under the floorboards somewhere. The usual stuff. Some folks in town believed it."

"Judging by the body temperature, he's been dead about twelve hours," said Haledjian. "In lay terms, he died of plain old age. Incidentally, who found the body?"

"Jim Casey, when he delivered the mail half an hour ago."

Haledjian stepped to the table where the sheriff had laid out the articles found in the dead man's pockets. There were two small fish for the cats, an antique pocket watch, and a dollar and ten cents in coins.

Haledjian picked up the fish, sniffed, and swiftly passed them a foot under the sheriff's nose. "Smell anything extraordinary?"

"No — just a faint fishy odor."

"That's what is extraordinary," replied Haledjian. "I'll have to request an autopsy, Sheriff. Old Carl's death is not what it appears!"

What was the basis for Haledjian's request?

After being twelve hours in Old Carl's pocket on a hot day, the fish would have smelled to high heaven.

Haledjian suspected that the nearly empty deep freeze (last trip to town seven weeks ago) had been used to lower the old man's body temperature quickly. Thus death was made to appear as occurring hours earlier.

The Case of the
Impoverished Artist

The body of Monroe Sheld, an impoverished sixty-year-old painter, lay over a table in his sweltering one-room apartment. A bullet had entered his right temple. On his right side, by the leg of his chair, was an old-fashioned, single-action revolver.

The table was bare except for a cracked plate, a saucerless cup, knife, fork, and spoon, and an overturned salt shaker.

"Sheld has been peddling his sketches for a dollar or two in the local bars," said Inspector Winters. "His doctor says he was stricken with heart failure two months ago and nearly died. You might say he ate a last meal and committed suicide."

"Correction," said Dr. Haledjian. "There was a bit about him in today's paper. A small but fashionable art gallery announced a one-man showing of his paintings next month. He had everything to live for."

Haledjian opened a small cupboard layered with dust. One plate and cup, and a setting of cheap silverware, however, were quite clean. Next he opened a paper garbage bag and sniffed.

"This food was put in the bag within the past three hours, or about the time of Sheld's death," asserted Haledjian. "Longer than that and it would have begun to spoil and smell in this heat."

Haledjian shut the bag. "I shouldn't close the case quite yet, Inspector. Sheld had a dinner guest who tried to cover up his presence here."

What made Haledjian so certain?

Sheld, having suffered a heart failure, would have watched his diet carefully. He never would have brought salt to the table unless it was for another's use.

The Case of the
Initialed Tie Clasp

Leo Murtag had been floating in the East River for three days when his corpse was fished out by the police.

"Whoever killed him nearly botched the job," Inspector Winters told a battery of reporters. "The killer first attempted to strangle him with Murtag's own bow tie. Apparently when that didn't work, he resorted to a forty-inch piece of tarred hemp rope — the kind used for marine purposes. It did the job properly.

"Murtag's pockets were empty," the inspector continued. "When found, he had on a white shirt with French cuffs and blue trousers, but no jacket."

An hour after the first editions hit the streets, Nick the Nose was banging on the inspector's door. He had, as usual, information to peddle.

"I found this," the grimy little informer said. He held out a tie clasp fashioned in the shape of a cat-boat. On the back was engraved, "To LM from GB."

"LM is Leo Murtag and GB is Gina Bettina, his old flame," volunteered Nick.

"Could be Gina," conceded the inspector. "We'll never know. She committed suicide last month. Where'd you find the clasp?"

"That bit of information will cost you," snapped Nick. "I figure if you knew where he lost the clasp, you'd know where he was attacked, and if — "

"Enough!" roared the inspector. "I'll pay — with this!"

He drove the toe of his shoe into the seat of Nick's pants.

"He deserves worse," commented Haledjian, opening the door as Nick flew by.

Why was Nick given the boot?

Nick's tie clasp was obviously a fake clue. Murtag would not have used one, for he was wearing a bow tie when slain.

The Case of the
Italian Grocer

The death of Joseph Pastrono, a grocer, might have passed for suicide but for the keen eye of Dr. Haledjian.

Pastrono had come to America from Italy as a boy of nine years. His family being poor, he had left school in the fourth grade to go to work.

He had married and raised two sons. Although of limited education, he faithfully read the news every evening in an Italian language newspaper.

His body was found above his grocery store, in the tidy four-room apartment where he had lived alone since the death of his wife Anna the year before. He had apparently shot himself with the revolver he usually kept in his store for protection.

The police found no substance to the rumors that he had hidden his life savings somewhere in his apartment.

Beside Pastrono's body was a suicide note, written, his sons were convinced, in his handwriting. It read:

"I am tired and sick. My body pains me every hour of the day. The doctors say nothing can be done; I am too old. If I were twenty years younger, I'd try to go on. But my Anna is dead, and my sons have families of their own. I do not wish to be a nuisance. This is the only solution for me. God forgive me!"

Haledjian put down the note and said, "Pastrono was murdered!"

How did he know?

Haledjian perceived at once that the note was a forgery.

Pastrono, who had left school in the fourth grade and read an Italian newspaper instead of one in English, could not have written a note perfect in grammar (including the subjunctive mode), punctuation, and spelling!

364

The Case of the
Italian Sports Car

"Two days ago somebody with a dime-store mask tried to stick up the City Bank," said Sheriff Monahan.

"The hold-up man panicked and fled empty-handed," he added. "It must have been the heat that made him try it."

Dr. Haledjian glanced out the open window of the patrol car. "The weather seems normal for October."

"Today is like the rest of the twelve days of the month — sixty degrees," said the sheriff. "But yesterday and the day before — whew! It was a hundred degrees, and folks went batty."

The sheriff drew up in front of a pretentious home.

"The Vandergriffs's mansion," he explained. "Their son Ted is a suspect in the holdup attempt. A woman near the bank saw him driving his Italian sports car away at a breakneck speed. I thought you'd be interested in his story."

Ted, a long-haired teenager, insisted the witness had been seeing heat waves near the bank, not him.

"Nobody's driven this job in a week," he said. "I've been using the family Rolls."

"An Italian sports car with American luxury," commented Haledjian, noting the sports car's radio, air-conditioner, heater, and power windows.

"Power brakes and power steering too," said Ted. "Why not? It cost my father a cool ten grand."

Haledjian slid behind the wheel and started the engine.

Ted's face went white as a sudden noise from inside the car swept away his alibi.

Can you guess the noise?

A blast of air — from the air-conditioner. Ted had forgotten to turn it off. Despite his denial, he had obviously used the car during the two-day heat wave when the attempted bank holdup had occurred!

The Case of the
Kidnapped Brother

Jerry Hickman gazed dully across the room as Inspector Winters and Dr. Haledjian sought to question him.

"I know it's difficult," said the inspector patiently. "But try to remember everything you can. You may give us a clue to your kidnappers."

Hickman shook his head regretfully. "What I remember isn't much. Three men jumped me Wednesday night in front of my apartment. They shoved me into a car and chloroformed me.

"The next thing I knew I was lying on a stone floor. I lit a match and saw I was in a windowless room empty except for a chair and a cracked sink. The door was locked.

"I could hear the kidnappers talking. I learned they had asked my stepsister Harriet for fifty thousand dollars. I guess they'd read that she'd just inherited our father's estate, valued at half a million dollars.

"After a few hours, they left to collect the ransom. I tried yelling, but it was no use. I couldn't batter down the door. I thought to lift it off its hinges, but it hinged on the other side. There was nothing to do but wait.

"When the men returned, I could tell they'd been successful in collecting the ransom. And I felt sure they now intended to kill me. The ones called Frank and Monty went for the car. The one called Beno came for me.

"I hid behind the door as Beno pushed it cautiously into the room. He had a flashlight and gun, and I almost got to him with the upraised chair when he dodged. He must have cracked me with the gun. I don't remember anything till I regained consciousness outside Harriet's home three hours ago."

"A good thing the ransom bills were marked," Haledjian told the inspector after the interview. "As soon as Hickman spends some of them, you can arrest him for fraud."

Why did Haledjian believe the kidnapping was staged?

Hickman said the door "hinged on the other side," and yet Beno "pushed it cautiously into the room." — a contradiction.
Beno would have pulled the door to himself, not pushed it into the room, since doors swing toward their hinged side.

The Case of the
Killer Dog

"It's so cold in here, there's no telling how long the old man's been dead," said Haledjian, turning to look out the window upon the snow-covered slopes.

Three sets of footprints led to the cabin's door. From the south came the double tracks newly made by himself and Sheriff Monahan.

From the north were the tracks of a single visitor. They led up to the door and away from it.

All about were the paw prints of a huge dog.

"Those tracks to the north are Buff Carter's, I take it," said Haledjian.

"Correct," said the sheriff. "Buff brought old Jed's supplies about once a week. He said his last trip here was six days ago, right after the big snow. He got inside the door, he says, when Jed's mongrel attacked him. Buff swears he won't be back till Jed gets rid of the beast."

"Buff won't have any reason to come back," muttered Haledjian, looking down at the half-naked body of Jed Tompkins.

"He must have been changing his clothes when his dog went loco and did that to his throat," mused the sheriff.

"Didn't Jed go outside?" asked Haledjian.

"Not since last September — that's when he broke his legs," answered the sheriff.

Suddenly Haledjian saw a great, ugly dog following Buff Carter's tracks toward the cabin. The animal moved with its nose to the snow for several hundred feet.

"That dog is big enough," said Haledjian. "But I doubt if a dog did the killing."

What aroused Haledjian's suspicion?

Buff Carter had claimed his "last trip . . . was six days ago," and yet his tracks were fresh enough to hold human odor. Had they been six days old, the dog would not have been sniffing them.

Haledjian believed Buff had staged the killing to make it appear as if the dog were the culprit.

The Case of the
Lakeside Murder

"I need your opinion on the Topping murder," Sheriff Monahan said to Dr. Haledjian.

"Topping was the guest of Arthur Blair," began the sheriff. "The Blair cottage is about a quarter mile from mine on Lake Gentsch. Two nights ago, as I was retiring, I heard a shot from there.

"Hurrying outside, I met Blair running toward me. 'Come quickly!' he cried. 'Fritz Topping's been shot!'

"As we started for his place, Blair told me, 'Fritz and I were watching the late news on television when all of a sudden the lights went out. I started to investigate when the front door swung open. A man with a rifle shot Fritz and disappeared before I could recover my wits.

"I saw Fritz had been shot in the heart and I ran directly to fetch you,' concluded Blair.

"The Blair cottage," the sheriff went on, "was

dark. A little moonlight played in the living room where Fritz Topping sat in the chair. I had brought a flashlight and it took but an instant to confirm that he was dead.

"Somebody had pulled the master fuse in the garage. When we replaced it, the kitchen light and a table lamp behind the corpse went on. I could see the body was slightly tilted away from the front door.

"I told Blair to try to recall what he could.

"The cottage was silent for a full minute before Blair shook his head. 'I-it happened so fast. I've told you everything I can remember.' "

"Which," broke in Haledjian, "should be enough to bring him to trial for murder!"

Why?

Blair claimed that he and Topping had been watching television when the lights went out and the murder occurred. Yet when the master fuse was replaced, there was a "full minute" of silence in the cottage.

Had Blair been telling the truth, the television would have come back on with the lights.

The Case of the
Lobster Joint

In the kitchen of his restaurant, The Lobster Joint, the body of Al Peltz lay covered by a police blanket.

"Al was too generous," sobbed Mrs. Peltz, wife of the murdered man. "He fed every hobo who came to the door."

"We think robbery was the motive," said Sheriff Monahan gently. "Your husband's pockets were empty. Did he normally carry a lot of cash?"

"About two hundred dollars," replied Mrs. Peltz. "I think that fellow in the khaki shirt must have done this terrible thing. Five minutes before I discovered Al's body, I came into the kitchen to pick up an order for table six. Al was talking to this man — why, that's him!"

An unshaven little man wearing a dirty khaki shirt suddenly broke away from the crowd of curious onlookers outside the kitchen door. The sheriff shouted to a deputy who collared the fugitive and hauled him before Mrs. Peltz.

"Look, lady, I was here," the man gasped in fright. "But I didn't do nothin'. The fella with the apron said he'd give me something to eat. He put a big red lobster into the pan and told me to come back in twenty minutes."

"C'mon!" snapped the sheriff. "You realized that Mrs. Peltz had seen you, and that we'd comb the county for you. A nice bluff coming back here. Now where did you hide the money?"

"I don't know nothin' about any money!" wailed the man. "I wouldn't lie."

"What innocent person needs to," said Haledjian with a sigh. "And yet a whopper has been told in this room!"

Who lied?

The man in khaki lied when he said Al "put a big red lobster into the pan." Lobsters turn red only after they've been boiled, and Al would not have boiled a lobster twice.

374

The Case of the
Manufacturer's Clothes

The body of T.B. Dowd, a manufacturer of men's hats, was found by two students in his expensive sports car parked in secluded Meadowlark Lane.

"Dowd was a lefty," Inspector Winters told Dr. Haledjian the next day at headquarters. "He apparently committed suicide.

"The bullet entered his left temple. When found, he was leaning over the steering wheel, slightly to the right of center. The pistol was on the floor by the clutch pedal."

Haledjian nodded thoughtfully and continued to study the pile of clothing which Dowd had been wearing.

On the police table were a pair of shiny black shoes, navy stretch socks, a blue suit, black leather belt, monogrammed underwear and shirt, a conservative tie, and two handkerchiefs — one soiled and one still folded for the breast pocket.

The inspector went on.

"Besides these clothes and the gun, the only other object in the car was a briefcase. It contained his firm's latest promotion campaign.

"Dowd told his secretary he was driving to Convention Hall to attend the menswear trade fair. He left his office at one P.M. The coroner places the time of his death around two-thirty P.M.

"He's supposed to be happily married and a financial success," concluded the inspector. "So why suicide?"

"It wasn't suicide," corrected Haledjian.

"The killer shot Dowd somewhere else, then staged the suicide in the parked car. But he forgot one item that gave the business away!"

What?

A manufacturer of men's hats, Dowd would never have gone to a menswear convention hatless, and no hat was found in the car!

The Case of the
Missing Model

"Jane left the house at three o'clock yesterday for the doctor's office," said her father. "She never came home. Her valise is still upstairs in her room, fully packed."

"She had planned on a trip?" asked Haledjian.

"To Mexico. Jane's a fashion model. She was to take part in a big fashion show in Mexico tomorrow. Her appointment with the doctor was for a vaccination."

"Did she keep it?"

"Well, I don't rightly know what doctor she went to, but she must have seen one."

"How can you be sure of that?"

"Charles Motley says so. I mean, he overheard Jane make a remark to that effect. Charlie lives next door, and about five o'clock as he was returning from work, he saw Jane and a man arguing near the bus stop on Weaver Street. The man gripped Jane's arm.

377

She pulled away, protesting, 'Don't, Ramon. I've just been vaccinated there. Stop it, you're hurting me!' "

"Didn't Charlie assist her?"

The father shifted uncomfortably. "Jane broke off her engagement with Charlie last month. I suppose he was still brooding. He saw this man and Jane enter a car and drive off. He didn't think it important till he learned Jane had vanished. Now he won't forgive himself for not helping her."

"Can Charlie describe the man with Jane?"

"A slight man with a waxed mustache. Wore a dark gray overcoat that fitted too tight. Charlie thinks he's seen the fellow with Jane before."

Haledjian pursed his lips and reached for the telephone. "Inspector Winters will want to have a long, long talk with Mr. Charlie Motley!"

Why did Haledjian doubt the ex-fiance's story?

Charlie Motley's slip was in stating that Jane had been hurt when the man gripped her vaccinated arm.

A fashion model, who often must wear sleeveless creations, would never disfigure her arm with a vaccination mark. She'd be vaccinated on the hip.

The Case of the
Mistaken Shot

Shortly after midnight, Dr. Haledjian received a call from Brad Worth pleading for help. Worth said he had just shot a man.

Arriving ten minutes later at Worth's beach house, the sleuth found a man lying face down a few paces inside the door.

"He's dead — don't touch him!" exclaimed Worth. "I've called the police. It was a mistake. He's my friend, Bill Mills!"

"All right, what happened?" asked Haledjian.

"Yesterday," began Worth, "an old classmate of mine, Chet Henry, came to see me. Chet is deaf, but he can read lips from an amazing distance.

"Chet wrote out a report for me. It said that around noon yesterday he noticed two men standing with their hands in their pockets, looking at my house. They spoke in whispers, and Chet, thinking this rather strange, stopped and observed them.

"Reading their lips, Chet learned that they planned to rob me of the Picasso hanging there."

Haledjian asked, "Why didn't you call the police then?"

"I was skeptical," said Worth remorsefully. "But an hour ago I heard the door open. I challenged the intruder. I thought he was pulling a gun, so I shot him. When I turned on the lights, I-I saw it was poor Bill Mills!"

"Very sad," said Haledjian, giving the "corpse" a gentle kick. "Okay, you can get up now. It was a good try at fooling an old detective."

Why didn't Haledjian believe the story?

Worth said that Chet Henry was attracted to the men because they were whispering. But as Henry was deaf, he couldn't have told whether they were whispering or shouting.

380

The Case of the
Mona Lisa

Bertie Tilford, England's gift to the international get-rich-quick set, decanted Dr. Haledjian's best brandy and sniffed critically.

Haledjian prepared himself for the latest of Bertie's money-making schemes.

"It is true," began Bertie, "that in the past I have asked you for money for enterprises which — I shall confess it! — were not quite proper. But now I've a chance at something big — da Vinci's Mona Lisa!"

"I thought the painting is in Paris," said the sleuth.

"Ha! So does the world!" exclaimed Bertie. "You will remember it was stolen in 1911. The painting which the authorities recovered was really a forgery by the superb Japanese counterfeiter, Yakki Yakameko.

"The genuine Mona Lisa was hidden in Tokyo till a buyer was found. Now it is coming to Texas, rolled up in a bolt of finest silk and shipped unwittingly by one of Japan's most reputable mills.

"I would not be a party to any criminal venture," Bertie hastily assured the sleuth. "I have, however, a contact who guarantees me that he can intercept the silk shipment and recover the painting. He needs only $30,000 to bribe the ruffians who guard it. The French will pay a reward of $1,000,000 for its recovery, I'm positive.

"If you could advance me the $30,000, dear boy," concluded Bertie. "I can personally promise you half the reward!"

"You won't get thirty cents," snapped Haledjian. *How come?*

The real Mona Lisa could not be "rolled up in a bolt of the finest silk." It is painted on wood!

The Case of the
Murdered Vocalist

The day after Dr. Haledjian was asked to solve the murder of singer Joy April, the international recording star, he was visited by Miss April's gray-haired manager, Chuck Petri.

"Miss April kept a most interesting record hidden in her vanity table," said Haledjian as the two men took seats in the library. "It was apparently her little secret. Did you know about it?"

"No," said Petri with a worried look.

"A detective found it in the false bottom of the vanity," said Haledjian. "The theory is that the killer was searching her apartment for it when she surprised him, and he stabbed her with a letter opener. Are you at all interested in it?"

"O-of course. Do you have it?" asked Petri.

"Yes, and I don't blame Miss April for keeping it hidden," said Haledjian. "It's not exactly for public consumption."

As the sleuth opened the middle drawer of his desk, he saw Petri put on his eyeglasses, a movement the manager made awkwardly because of the bandages on his thumb and forefinger.

"Ah," said Haledjian, lifting out a leather-bound diary. "Miss April started it May 12. The last entry is the day of her death. She put down everything that happened in her life during those months, and you don't come off very well!"

"You can bet everything about me are lies," snarled Petri. "I hated her, all right. But I didn't kill her!"

"Perhaps not," retorted Haledjian. "But you'll have a lot of explaining to do to convince the police."

How come?

When Haledjian mentioned the "interesting record" kept by Joy April, the singer, Petri put on his eyeglasses — and fell into Haledjian's trap!

Had Petri really known nothing about the secret diary, as he claimed, the word "record" should have indicated something to be heard, not read!

The Case of the
Nature Lover

On the night of June 18, Matthew Reynolds, a Wall Street broker, was shot to death in his duplex apartment. The police immediately threw out a dragnet for Bill McKay, who had publicly sworn "to get" Reynolds.

"Reynolds testified against McKay when McKay was sentenced for income tax evasion. He recently finished serving a year term in prison," Inspector Winters told Dr. Haledjian as the pair drove upstate ten days after the murder.

"Yesterday," continued the inspector, "a hiker came upon McKay camping out. McKay claims to have been there since his release from prison a month ago. He hadn't heard about Reynold's death, he said.

"He gave himself up to the local authorities voluntarily," continued the inspector. "I asked Sheriff Patch to guide us to McKay's campsite."

The sheriff's car was waiting on the side of the highway. He led the way over the rutty back roads as far as the two cars could travel.

Proceeding on foot, they tramped for miles back into the green hills, arriving finally at a tent pitched on a grassy meadow.

"McKay claims he has lived in this tent on this meadow for a month," said the sheriff. "He could have too, for all anyone ever comes by this spot."

"The airtight alibi," said Haledjian, ducking into the tent.

Two metallic objects glinted on the green grass by McKay's cot.

"Rifle shells, the same caliber used in killing Reynolds," said Haledjian. "You can take us to McKay now, sheriff. He's going to need a new alibi!"

Why?

McKay claimed he had lived in the tent for a month. Yet inside the tent the grass was still "green."

After a month under canvas, the grass inside the tent would have withered to brown.

The Case of the
New Year's Eve Murder

Mugsy Flynn scowled at Inspector Winters and Dr. Haledjian. "You got nothin' on me," he snarled. "I hated Dee Dee McGhie, but I didn't bump him off New Year's Eve."

The inspector calmly met Mugsy's belligerent gaze. "We have a doorman who is pretty sure it was you who stepped from behind a parked car on Fifty-third Street and shot Dee Dee at five minutes before midnight."

"I was in a nightclub till after midnight!" bawled Mugsy. "I didn't come outside till everybody was huggin' and shoutin' 'Happy New Year!' "

"What made you leave just when the fun was really getting started?" demanded the inspector suspiciously.

"The dance band. They whooped up some rock 'n roll bit as the clock struck twelve. So I got up and left. That kinda music reminds me of my wife. Anyway, I hit the street and I remember lookin' at my watch — a minute after midnight. I saw a crowd collectin' — "

"What club did you leave?"

"How should I know? The street is full of joints. I guess maybe I was in half a dozen between ten and midnight. Say, come to think of it, I bet it was the Blue Door I was in."

"The bartender at the Blue Door remembers seeing Mugsy, but he can't be sure of the exact time," the inspector said to Haledjian after Mugsy was ushered from the office.

"You won't need the bartender's testimony if you can get Mugsy to sign the remarks he just made," answered the sleuth. "His own words destroy his alibi."

What words?

Mugsy claimed the band "whooped up some rock 'n roll just as the clock struck twelve," in order to prove he was inside and not on the street when Dee Dee was killed. To Mugsy's sorrow, there is only one song played across America at midnight on New Year's Eve, and it's not rock 'n roll. It's "Auld Lang Syne."

The Case of the
Old-Fashioned Pen

Rodney Stites, professor of French at State University, lay slumped across his desk, an apparent suicide.

"I heard the shot about an hour ago," said Carl, the manservant. "I rushed in and called you right away."

Dr. Haledjian walked to the desk, situated in the middle of the professor's library. "Touch anything?"

"Nothing except the telephone," was the reply.

Haledjian examined the body. Death, which had occurred within the hour, was due to a bullet fired into the right temple at extremely close range.

A thirty-two caliber pistol lay on the thick carpet to the right of the professor's head. On the desk was a note. Written in ink, with several splotches, it read: "I can't go on without Elsie."

"Elsie, his wife, ran off with a young artist last year," Haledjian mused.

He turned his attention to the old-fashioned quill pen clutched in the deceased's right hand. An open, antique inkwell stood next to the desk phone an inch from the pen point.

On the stand of the inkwell was engraved: "For Rodney on our Tenth Anniversary. Love Elsie."

"Call the police," Haledjian told Carl. "The suicide note has to be a fake. This is clearly a case of murder!"

How come?

The murderer blundered in arranging the death scene. The professor could not have fired the gun into his right temple. His right hand still held the pen.

The Case of the
Overheard Gunshot

"I'm having trouble with Clara's — "

Dr. Haledjian heard Ted Felton's frantic voice at the other end of the telephone terminated by the sound of a gunshot.

Hurrying to Felton's bachelor apartment, he found the door unlocked. Felton lay on his stomach in the dining area, a yard from the dangling telephone receiver.

He had been shot from behind. The bullet had entered below the shoulder blade and emerged, Haledjian saw upon turning the body on its back, at the left breast.

Blood stained Felton's white silk shirt around the bullet's points of entry and exit. The only other blood was a small stain on the floor, and it was made all but invisible by the red carpet.

As Haledjian began a search for the bullet, he heard a gasp. A blonde girl stood in the doorway, her eyes wide. Haledjian introduced himself and explained his presence.

"I'm Clara Blakeless, Ted's fiancée," she said falteringly. "W-who did it?"

"Have you an idea?" Haledjian parried.

"Ernie Matte," replied Clara vindictively. "He's been mad with jealousy since I broke my engagement to him last month."

"Did he ever threaten Ted?"

"I don't know. But he threatened me. It would be like him to shoot Ted in the back. He's such a coward!"

"Ernie Matte may be a coward," said Haledjian. "But I doubt that he shot Ted."

How come?

Haledjian suspected Clara, who knew Ted Felton had been shot in the back.

Since the corpse lay on its back, she should have assumed, had she been innocent, that the blood-stained wound on the left breast was the bullet's point of entry and not its exit.

The Case of the
Parked Car

The waiter touched a match to Dr. Haledjian's order of Cherries Jubilee. Instantly, a blue flame sprouted from the dish.

"Puts me in mind of poor Walt Dahlgren," said Haledjian soberly.

"The movie magnate who took his own life last week?" inquired Octavia, his fair dinner companion.

"The manner of Dahlgren's death is still unsettled," pointed out Haledjian. "I'll tell you the important facts and let you be the detective.

"Dahlgren was found behind the wheel of his sedan. The car was parked on the grass of the Grenwich Parkway just below the Stillford exit.

"Death was due to a thirty-two caliber bullet which had entered at the right temple. A single-shot, thirty-two pistol lay near the accelerator pedal.

"The sedan was spotless, inside and out. A careful

search — by vacuum cleaners — of the ground within twenty feet of the parked car disclosed only two apple cores, a stub of a week-old theater ticket, and a rusted earring.

"Dahlgren's were the only fingerprints found on the pistol. An autopsy showed powder burns at the wound area and fresh cherries in his mouth and digestive system. He must have been eating the fruit up to the instant of his death.

"Now," concluded Haledjian. "Can you tell me why I think Dahlgren was not a suicide, but had been killed elsewhere and brought to the spot where he was found?"

Octavia couldn't. Can you?

Dahlgren had been eating fresh cherries "up to the instant of his death." Yet the interior of the car was "spotless," and the ground about failed to disclose what should have been there.
Cherry pits.

The Case of the
Phony Cop

"I represent Franklin D. Van Clausand II," said Godwin, the attorney, settling himself in Dr. Haledjian's study. "The young man is being framed for robbery and murder. I'm hopeful you can clear him.

"Franklin has been working for a year in one of his father's banks," continued the attorney. "Last Tuesday, before the doors opened, a man dressed as a police officer gained admission. He looked like a motorcycle cop — black leather jacket, boots, sun goggles, and white crash helmet. He even had a badge.

"Franklin was closing the vault when the phony cop drew a pistol. Putting the muzzle against Franklin's neck, he forced him to fill a sack with bills of high denomination.

"As the thief was leaving, a guard drew his gun. Two shots were fired. The guard fell, dying.

"Franklin was able to provide the only description

of the killer. An alarm went out for a man about thirty years old, six feet tall, with fair complexion, blue eyes, and a crescent scar on his upper lip.

"That afternoon one Edgar Burgess was picked up over in Flint for speeding. He answered the description. And $300,000 was found in his car.

"When informed who had given out his description, Burgess grew furious. He tried to implicate young Franklin, insisting he was a partner in the crime."

The attorney paused. "Franklin swears he's never seen Burgess except once — in the bank. But he's come under a cloud of suspicion."

"And there he must stay," said Haledjian. "He was obviously an accomplice, but lost his nerve when Burgess killed the guard."

Why?

Franklin's description of Burgess was too good. As the "cop," Burgess wore sun goggles. Franklin could not have known his eyes were "blue" unless he had see him before.

The Case of the
Phony Crash

Dr. Haledjian had just turned over drowsily in his sleeping bag when he saw a big car come down the short dirt road, which fed off the highway, and disappear over the cliff.

Running after the car was a tall man. He stopped at the edge of the cliff, lay down on the ground, and began to moan and shout, "Help! Help! My back!"

Four other campers reached the man before the thoughtful sleuth.

Haledjian bypassed the group and descended to the car.

It was overturned and almost totally wrecked. About the only things intact were the four wornout tires, which still spun lazily.

Two days later Haledjian received Abbot, the insurance agent, who stated his difficulties.

"Starnes claims he fell asleep at the wheel and

woke up just in time to escape going over the cliff with the car.

"At first we thought he needed money in a hurry and wanted to collect his auto insurance. The car is only five days old and worth $6,500.

"It turns out he's claiming he can't work a lick — hurt his back. You know about injuries there. He has a big monthly income policy, and we think he's shamming.

"You're the only witness," concluded Abbot. "But Starnes's attorney will capitalize on the facts that it was night and you were barely awake, and therefore you didn't see clearly."

"You won't need my testimony," said Haledjian. "Starnes planned to wreck the car. That is obvious."

How come?

Starnes, like many who fake accidents, had removed the new tires from his "five-day-old" car and replaced them with "worn-out" ones.

The Case of the
Poisoned Drink

"We're holding Eddie Jordon on suspicion of murder," Inspector Winters told Dr. Haledjian. "Yesterday Jordon and Harry Lewis ate lunch together at a crowded restaurant. When and how Jordon slipped the poison into Lewis's drink in front of all those people is a mystery.

"Both men ordered club sandwiches and soft drinks," continued the inspector. "Just as the waiter brought the drinks, Lewis was summoned to the telephone. The receptionist says that Lewis complained to her that he'd picked up a dead line."

"You believe that the call was a decoy to allow Jordon a chance to poison the drink?" asked Haledjian.

"So it seems. We know the drinks were all right when they were brought to the table. The waiter admits it."

"Admits?"

"The waiter says Lewis ordered a root beer and Jordon a sarsaparilla. He placed the order in the kitchen, and when he returned to pick up the drinks, he didn't know which was which. The chef didn't remember either.

"In glasses, the two drinks look alike," went on the inspector. "The waiter admits he sipped one to find out which was which. He tasted the root beer, which Lewis ordered. That means the root beer wasn't poisoned till afterward, or the waiter would have been poisoned too."

"A kitchen is a busy place," said Haledjian. "It was easy for the waiter to slip the poison into the drink he served Lewis."

The inspector looked startled. "But — why?"

"Undoubtedly because somebody — perhaps Jordon — paid him well. You won't have any trouble. The waiter will confess once you confront him with his lie."

What was the waiter's lie?

The waiter claimed he established which drink should be served to Lewis and which to Jordon by sipping one — the root beer. However, it is impossible to distinguish root beer from sarsaparilla by taste.

The Case of the
Pudgy Playboy

It was the steadfast ambition of American toothpaste model Betti Allen, "the girl with the million-dollar smile," to acquire a corner of the wealth of Far Eastern playboy Abka Fazl.

Ungraciously, the pudgy Fazl was more bewitched by food than amour. So Betti was compelled to rest her charms and exercise her wits.

Over a table creaking with silver serving dishes the determined adventuress stared darkly as Fazl shoveled in crabmeat ravigotte.

At eight-thirty P.M. a waiter entered the suite and served the dessert — blueberry pie surmounted by avocado sherbert — and coffee.

Fazl gulped nearly all the dessert before mouthing a massive belch. Eyes rolling, he toppled off the chair.

Fifteen minutes later Betti's urgent call for a doctor fetched Dr. Haledjian, a guest at the hotel.

Betti admitted him to Fazl's suite. She was able to smile bravely, a flexion which not only demonstrated her wonderful pluck but also displayed her dazzling white teeth to full advantage. She opened her baby blue eyes wide and pointed.

Fazl lay on his back, burping drowsily.

Haledjian reported the episode to the police. "The piece of pie left on Fazl's plate contained knockout drops. Miss Allen said she ate all of hers before passing out, and so a test was impossible.

"What about Fazl's jewelry, stolen while the pair were unconscious?" asked the chief of police.

"That's a question for Miss Allen," replied Haledjian. "She was unquestionably in on the robbery."

How did Haledjian know?

Haledjian knew Betti Allen had not eaten the drugged blueberry pie, and therefore she was conscious during the robbery. If she had eaten it, her teeth "fifteen minutes later" would not have been "dazzling white."

They would have been stained blue from the berries.

The Case of the
Railroad Crash

On the night of July 15, the engineer of a west-bound local missed a signal and crashed head-on into the Rocket, a high-speed express out of Chicago.

The result — one of the bloodiest disasters in railroad history.

"It strikes me odd that all the serious casualties were in the first seven cars of both trains," said Dr. Haledjian. "All except one."

"Jess Fromm, you mean?" asked Inspector Winters. "What makes you question his death?"

"Partly because Fromm's niece asked me to investigate," replied Haldejian.

The inspector went to his files. "Fromm was on his way to a hardware convention with his business partner, Wendel Smith," said the inspector. "Here's Smith's statement.

"According to Smith, he and Fromm shared compartment C in the last car of the local. Seconds before the crash, Fromm got up and walked forward to the compartment's toilet.

"At the impact, Fromm was standing. He was thrown back and struck his head against the ridge of the card table set between the facing seats.

"Smith now owns the whole business," said the inspector. "There's your motive. Method? He could have struck Fromm in the back of the neck with the table AFTER the crash. But how are you going to prove it?"

"I should start," replied Haledjian, "with the obvious lie in Smith's statement."

What was Smith's lie?

Smith lied when he stated Fromm was "thrown back" at the impact.

Anyone standing, or sitting, in a speeding vehicle involved in a head-on crash is thrown forward at the instant of impact.

The Case of the
Shot in the Back

On a shivery November evening Dr. Haledjian was taking a constitutional when he heard a shot. He saw an elderly man suddenly lurch against the front door of a nearby house, fall, and lie motionless on the porch.

The two other men on the block joined the famous sleuth in sprinting to the prostrate man.

They found him dead, shot through the back.

After introducing himself, Haledjian snapped, "Each of you had better have an alibi. I'm sure one of you shot him and tossed the gun away. But the police will find it."

Both men, who were wearing gloves and tight overcoats, insisted they didn't know the deceased. Each claimed he was simply taking the evening air.

"I'm Ted Baggs," said the first man. "I noticed the dead man locking the front door a split second before I heard the shot. I ran right up to him."

"I'm Sid Cole," said the second man, who had reached the porch last. "I heard the shot, but I didn't know what happened till I saw you two running for the house."

The key was still in the front door. Haledjian turned it, entered the house, and called the police.

"The dead man's wife, Mrs. Trill, is an invalid," Haledjian told Inspector Winters twenty-five minutes later. "She says her husband was going out to the drugstore. He habitually locks the house when he leaves her alone."

"Any leads?" asked the inspector.

"Yes," declared Haledjian. "Arrest — "

Whom?

Ted Baggs — who knew Trill was locking (not unlocking) his front door.

Baggs must have been watching the house for a long time, otherwise he could not have known whether Trill was entering or leaving.

The Case of the
Silver Bowl

"I can't be certain from a photograph, but that looks like the gunman," said Fitzpatrick.

"Nose Cole," said Inspector Winters, glancing at the police album. "Two convictions for armed robbery. You say Cole entered the store just as it opened for the day?"

"That's right," replied Fitzpatrick. "I had my back to the door when I heard him enter. 'Don't turn around,' he commanded. 'I've got a gun, and I'll use it if I have to!' "

"Then what happened?"

"I did exactly as he told me. I passed all the silver to him from the wall showcase. I guess he put it into the bag I saw him carrying when he raced out the door."

"You saw his back," said Haledjian. "Did you ever see his face?"

"No. He made me pass each piece of silverware to him behind my back."

"Yet you claim to know what he looks like," interposed the inspector.

Fitzpatrick stiffened. "I saw his reflection. W-we keep the silver highly polished. As I passed him a large fruit bowl, I could see his image reflected on the inside of it. I saw him only for a few seconds. Maybe it wasn't Cole — "

"You seemed to be fairly certain a minute ago," snapped the inspector.

"Did you see the gun in the reflection?" Haledjian put in.

"Come to think of it, I didn't," admitted Fitzpatrick.

"You didn't see Cole, either. I suggest you return the silver you stole rather than continue this farce," admonished Haledjian. "It will go easier with you."

What was Fitzpatrick's blunder?

Fitzpatrick could never have made an identification of a gunman or anyone else on the basis of an image reflected briefly on the inside of a polished bowl. The inside of a bowl reflects images upside down.

The Case of the
Silver Pen

"The police were here all morning, darrhhhling! It's been simply frightful!"

Covering her face with her delicately lotioned hands, Vivian Hobson, Broadway's brightest — if oldest — ingenue, slumped onto a purple chaise longue.

Dr. Haledjian, an old friend, studied the bedroom, from which the actress's daughter Shari had been kidnapped the previous night.

A rope fashioned of bedsheets and blankets, and anchored to one bed leg, dangled from the window. It reached to within a yard of the ground some dozen feet below.

"The kidnapper must have sneaked into the house during the day, because everything is locked at night," said Vivian. "I was on the balcony around midnight when I saw a man work down the sheets. He had poor Shari across one shoulder, limp. He must have knocked her unconscious, the ruffian!"

"Has anything been moved in the room?" asked Haledjian.

"No, everything is precisely as it was."

Haledjian walked outside. On the street he found a newsboy and gave him half a dollar to retrace the kidnapper's route down the bedding.

As the lad swung out the window, the bed was dragged a few inches from its position against the wall, revealing a glittering object on the floor.

Haledjian bent over and picked up a silver fountain pen.

"Is it a clue?" exclaimed Vivian.

"Yes — a clue to a faked kidnapping," retorted Haledjian. "Your new play, 'The Kidnapped Daughter,' needs a bit of publicity. That's why you staged this, isn't it?"

How did Haledjian know?

Had there really been a kidnapping, the double load of kidnapper and girl pulling on the bedclothes would have dragged the bed away from the wall, as the weight of the newsboy did.

The Case of the
Spinning Eggs

The soda fountain was deserted except for Dr. Haledjian and a red-headed youngster engrossed in spinning an egg.

Suddenly the egg twirled off the counter and dropped out of Haledjian's sight. There was a small crash, and the boy's grin turned to a look of dismay.

The counterman, to whom broken eggs were a regular occurrence, passed him a dustpan and broom.

At this point Haledjian paid for his sundae and departed. The incident was forgotten until that evening, when it was recalled by a visit from two boys in quest of a detective.

"We spin eggs," explained Glenn Stewart. "Whoever's egg spins the longest wins."

"Red Mason's won everything. Bikes, skates, footballs. He never loses," moaned Larry Appleson. "You've got to help us discover how he does it!"

"You suspect foul play?" asked Haledjian, frowning. "Suppose you tell me where the eggs come from."

"We get them fresh from the farm," said Glenn. "Each boy chooses his egg and lets his opponent mark it with a pencil. On the day of the match, the eggs are examined. That way we can tell if it's the same egg, and if it's been doctored up."

"A difficult case," muttered Haledjian.

The next afternoon he witnessed an egg-spinning contest. The champion, Red Mason, turned out to be the boy he had seen practicing on the drugstore counter.

Red's egg easily spun the longest. Grinning smugly, he walked off with his opponent's baseball glove.

"That will be his last victory," Haledjian announced. "I've cracked this case!"

How?

The fact that the counterman had handed Red a broom instead of a mop or towel with which to clean up the broken egg had tipped Haledjian that Red's egg was hardboiled.

And a hardboiled egg will outspin a raw egg every time.

412

The Case of the
Stolen Pesos

Motoring through South America, Dr. Haledjian arrived in a mountain village as the local police were preparing to hang a man named Manuel Rodriguez.

The chief of police recognized Haledjian and promptly delayed the execution while he told the famous criminologist all about the case.

The previous month, said the chief, the national mint had been robbed of a million one-peso notes by a pair of masked men.

Three nights ago, Pedro Gonzales, a farmer, noticed a dim light in the window of an abandoned house near the village. Investigating, he saw two men seated by a candle, apparently arguing.

Pedro stopped outside of earshot, fearing to move too close. But he recognized one of the pair, Manuel Rodriguez, who had recently rented a room in his house. The next night, after Rodriquez went out, Pedro entered his room and found a new peso. Its serial number identified it as one of the stolen million.

Pedro immediately hurried to the abandoned house. This time he crept close enough to hear.

Rodriguez was in a temper. He insisted he had carefully counted his share again that afternoon and it wasn't half the loot — it was a thousand pesos short. The two men fought, and suddenly Rodriguez stabbed the other.

"I'm pretending to hang Rodriguez," whispered the police chief. "I want to scare him into telling me where he hid the million and the body of his partner."

"He can't tell you either," said Haledjian. "He's innocent. Pedro is trying to frame him."

How did Haledjian know?

Pedro's mistake was in declaring that Rodriguez said he had "carefully counted his share again that day." Impossible!

It would have taken Rodriguez at least five days — working around the clock — to count "half the loot," half of one million pesos!

The Case of the
Stranded Blonde

A look of satisfaction settled on young Harrington's face as he sat at dinner with Dr. Haledjian.

"Last week I put to good use my long association with you, Doctor." The handsome youth puffed a moment on his cigar. Then he related what had happened to him.

"I was driving my convertible up to Albany when night overtook me, still fifty miles from my destination. I thought I'd better double check my route, and so I inquired at a roadside tavern.

"While I was endeavoring to catch the bartender's eye, an extraordinarily beautiful woman sat down on the stool next to mine.

"She begged my forgiveness for speaking, and, quite covered with embarrassment, confessed she had left her purse on the bus. What could I do?

"After three rounds of martinis, she refused another drink, but demurely asked for a quarter for the bus home. 'Nonsense!' I protested and escorted her to my car.

"We had driven but a mile when a pair of headlights swung into the road behind me. The girl turned around and uttered a cry. 'My husband! He'll kill us both!'

"The road being dark and unfamiliar, I decided against a race. I pulled to the side and stopped. So did the black sedan following us. An enormous man jumped out, bellowing wrathfully. But I put an end to his posturing by pointing out the blunder in their plot. I drove off, leaving the pair of conspirators furious but far wiser."

"Congratulations," said Haledjian. "A simple case, but an instructive one. Henceforth you will be alert to the cunning behind a pretty face."

How did Harrington know he was being framed?

It is impossible to identify a car at night while looking back into its headlights. The girl could recognize the car which followed them only if she knew beforehand that it would be there.

The Case of the
Stunned Nephew

Dr. Haledjian knelt down to examine the spider which had spun a beautiful, wheel-shaped web across the lower half of the back door.

"A species of Argiopidae," said the sleuth.

"Uncle Phil would know its exact name," said young Bush. "He's sort of a bug himself. I-I mean he won't let me kill anything, even a rat. Look at this house — I can't even dust away the cobwebs for him."

"It's rather like a setting for a horror show," agreed Haledjian. "Suppose you tell me what happened here."

"Uncle Phil is in Europe on his sabbatical," began Bush, leading the way to the library. "He asked me to check the house once a week. I have the key to the front door.

"About an hour ago, I arrived to inspect the house. I heard noises as I entered.

"I called out. Suddenly a big man ran past me and out the back door. I might have caught him, but I tripped over a pile of bird-food cartons in the hall, stunning myself.

"When I recovered, the intruder was gone. I found the safe as you see it, open and empty. I telephoned you right away from the house next door."

"What was in the safe?" asked Haledjian.

"I've no idea, but I can write Uncle Phil. Here's his address," said Bush, producing a folded slip of paper.

Haledjian read: "Blue Lion Hotel, Harwick, Roxburgh, Scotland."

"Before you call the police," snapped the sleuth, "you had better improve your story!"

How come?

Had an intruder escaped by the back door, as Bush claimed, he would have broken apart the beautiful spider web.

The Case of the
Suicide Note

"I heard the shot at about nine-thirty," said Mathews, the secretary. "I found Mr. Southworth in his den exactly as you see him."

The famous playwright and Broadway producer was dead of a bullet fired from close range into his left temple. His left hand clutched a thirty-eight revolver, his right held a pen with which he had apparently written the suicide note lying on the desk in front of him.

Leaning over the dead man's shoulder, Dr. Haledjian read:

"I no longer possess the health and strength to perform the labours which once brought me joy. I have received all the honours and riches any man has a right to expect in one lifetime. Now, before I become a burden to my daughter, Alice, I wish to depart this wordly theatre."

"Is this in Mr. Southworth's handwriting?" asked Haledjian.

"I'm not an expert, sir, but it does resemble his," replied Mathews.

"How many persons have keys to the house?"

"I do, sir, and the cook. Then there's Miss Alice, and Mr. Arnold."

"Who is he?"

"Mr. Arnold Southworth, a younger brother. He arrived from England for a visit and occupies the guest bedroom."

"Did the brothers ever quarrel?"

"On the contrary, they hit it off first rate. Mr. Arnold wanted Mr. Vernon to accompany him back to England this summer. When their parents were divorced, Mr. Arnold was reared in London by the father. Mr. Vernon remained with his mother in America."

"Did Vernon say he would go to England?"

"I don't believe he'd quite made up his mind. They discussed it again tonight, just before Mr. Arnold left for a dinner engagement."

"I shall be interested to hear Arnold's alibi for this evening," said Haledjian. "Vernon never wrote the suicide note."

How did Haledjian reach his conclusion?

Three words in the note, "labour," "honours," and "theatre," reveal an invariable English spelling preference. Vernon, the American, would have written "labor," "honors," and "theater."

The Case of the
Uneasy Squirrel

The day after the Valley Park Bank had been robbed of $28,000 by three men, police arrested Phil Lott, a guard at the bank.

Lott had been under surveillance as the possible "inside man" in the robbery. He was caught with a birdhouse stuffed with $7,000, exactly a quarter of the loot.

"Lott insists he found the birdhouse by chance," Inspector Winters told Dr. Haledjian. "I want you to hear his story."

Lott was ushered into the inspector's office. After protesting his innocence, he repeated this story.

"Every day I eat my lunch at the park across the street from the bank," he began. "I always sit in the same secluded spot.

"I was feeding the pigeons when I noticed a squirrel on a tree, halfway between the ground and the lowest branch.

"Slowly, as if something in the branches made him uneasy, the squirrel backed down the trunk, reached the ground, turned, and scampered off.

"I walked to the tree, curious. Among the branches I saw a birdhouse which looked new to me. I climbed up and saw an oilcloth inside it.

"I took the birdhouse down to examine it. That's when two men grabbed me. I never got my hand inside. But they found all that money in the oilcloth and arrested me. I'm innocent!"

After Lott had departed, the inspector said. "We're sure the money was Lott's payoff. But we can't crack that nutty story."

"Oh, yes, you can," replied Haledjian.

How?

Lott claimed that it was the curious action of the squirrel backing down the tree trunk that led to his discovery of the birdhouse. A lie! Squirrels invariably descend a tree headfirst!

ABOUT THE AUTHOR

DONALD J. SOBOL has written sixty books for young readers, including more than twenty-five about Encyclopedia Brown. Among his numerous awards, he received a special Edgar Allan Poe Award from the Mystery Writers of America for his contribution to mystery writing.

Mr. Sobol was born in New York City and attended Oberlin College in Oberlin, Ohio. He lives in Miami, Florida, with his wife.